AROUND THE WORLD IN 80 WORDS

CREATIVE WRITING COMPETITION FOR 7-11 YEAR-OLDS

The West Midlands

Edited by Donna Samworth

First published in Great Britain in 2013 by:

 Young**Writers**

Remus House
Coltsfoot Drive
Peterborough
PE2 9BF
Telephone: 01733 890066
Website: www.youngwriters.co.uk

Printed and bound in the UK by BookPrintingUK
Website: www.bookprintinguk.com

Foreword

Since Young Writers was established in 1990, our aim has
been to promote and encourage written creativity amongst
children and young adults. By giving aspiring young authors
the chance to be published, Young Writers effectively
nurtures the creative talents of the next generation,
allowing their confidence and writing ability to grow.

With our latest fun competition, *Around The World In
80 Words,* primary school children nationwide were
given the tricky challenge of writing a story with a
beginning, middle and an end in just eighty words.

The diverse and imaginative range of entries made
the selection process a difficult but enjoyable task
with stories chosen on the basis of style, expression,
flair and technical skill. A fascinating glimpse into
the imaginations of the future, we hope you will
agree that this entertaining collection is one that
will amuse and inspire the whole family.

Contents

Woodthorpe Primary School, Birmingham

The Stories

THE GREAT CHASE

Jumping from vine to vine, Rodriguez, the photographer, was hunting for wildlife animals because he was a Mexican wildlife photographer. Rodriguez was also searching for the deadliest sabre-toothed tiger that had ever existed in the world! Rodriguez found slimy lizards, elegant deer, snappy alligators and scratchy koala bears. Finally he found the death blazing red-eyed devil, the sabre-toothed tiger! *Snap!* He took a picture. 'Oh no!' Rodriguez blinded the tiger. *Roar!* the tiger screeched …

Lewis Broadstock (10)
Glebefields Primary School, Tipton

THE MIGHTY JUNGLE

Ricardo, who was a Spanish wildlife photographer, was hunting for the deadly white tiger. After years of searching Ricardo finally met it. *Snap!* Suddenly he took a picture. The flash made him angry, therefore Ricardo was petrified and sprinted rapidly for his life! Dodging branches incessantly, leaping over rough twigs, haphazardly! He was running too fast so he began panting heavily, fingertips away from the waterfall. It was as flowing as the wind. Did he jump in?

Charlie Cox
Glebefields Primary School, Tipton

THE HORRIFYING JUNGLE

As always, Martin was taking photographs in the jungle, he was a fantastic photographer. Martin was wearing cool summer shorts and a cool summer shirt. He was brave, he was always going to the jungle. He was going to find a dreadful tiger, instead he found a talking monkey. Gradually Martin had seen a Bengal tiger too! He took the picture, it furiously ran towards him! Martin ran, panting heavily, he tripped over a branch and fell into a pond …

Cameron Payne
Glebefields Primary School, Tipton

SNAP

After twenty-two years of searching, finally James the professional wildlife photographer had come across the magnificent animal he most desperately wanted to snap, the dreaded tiger! As he got ready to take the photo, his long dark brown hair fell in front of the shiny, diamond black lens. Unfortunately for James he pressed take and the flash had flashed in the tiger's blue eyes. The chase was on! James was heading for the rapid, unsafe waterfall! *Splash* …

Jack McKnight (11)
Glebefields Primary School, Tipton

UNTITLED

Bobby, who was a middle-aged man, was in the peaceful jungle looking for monkeys to kidnap for Dudley zoo. All of a sudden he found two cute cubs. As he rapidly grabbed them, the mother monkey appeared. 'Run!' Without a second thought he speedily sprinted, holding the two horrified cubs. Unsurprisingly he sprinted whilst the fearful monkey was chasing him. Suddenly he arrived at a spiky pit! Realising he was trapped, he thought *what shall I do?*

Macaulay Steventon
Glebefields Primary School, Tipton

IN THE JUNGLE!

Dashing rapidly through the emerald, smooth vines was Chere Storm! She was alarmed at all the horrifying, weird noises! Besides this, there was a vindictive, vicious tiger that Chere spotted and was briskly chasing her! Although it was happening, she still stopped and looked behind. She came to a gushing, baby blue waterfall. Leaping like a frog through the waterfall, she amazingly reached a rocky cave. She was so relieved, she sighed triumphantly! She got the golden sword and *slash …!*

Shyann Allsopp
Glebefields Primary School, Tipton

UNTITLED

Suddenly the old purple plane started to lose fuel. Then quickly it shook because the useless engines stopped. Captain Will screamed in terror as the tiny plane began to crash. When it hit the ground Will got knocked out.

After a while Will woke up. He saw a hairy monkey swinging swiftly across the green trees. The scared, fearful monkey jumped on his back. Suddenly the monkey started to be his best friend!

Louis Nightingale (10)
Glebefields Primary School, Tipton

CAPTAIN WILL'S GREAT ADVENTURE

Suddenly the old purple aeroplane started to lose fuel. Then it shook slowly because the useless engine stopped! Captain Will screamed, terrified as the tiny plane began to crash. When it hit the ground Will got knocked out!

After a while he woke up and he saw colourful birds flying gently throughout the colossal trees. Then he stood up and he had a look around. Will looked behind the tree, he could see … a tiger. The tiger chased, Will escaped.

Ellie Price (10)
Glebefields Primary School, Tipton

UNTITLED

Suddenly the old purple aeroplane started to lose fuel. Then it shook slowly because the useless engine stopped! Captain Will screamed fearfully as the tiny aeroplane began to crash. When it hit the ground Will got knocked out.

After a while he woke up and he saw colourful birds flying quickly through the wonderful trees. Then he stood up with a nice smile on his face. Then an evil black lion was on a branch by him and scared him.

Demi Selwood (10)
Glebefields Primary School, Tipton

THE TIGER CHASE

In a deep, dark jungle there was a man called Bruce Wayne, who had eyes as blue as the sky. While prickly leaves fell on the damp ground, however the green vines dangled everywhere.

Two minutes later, *crack!* A twig. *Roar!* went a tough Bengal tiger so he ran rapidly whilst in fear. Although he was hanging on the edge of a waterfall, the Bengal tiger was a few paces behind so he jumped quickly into an endless sparkling river …

Owen-Lee Howell (10)
Glebefields Primary School, Tipton

5

THE QUEST FOR THE GOLDEN SWORD

However timid Lillian was, she was determined to find the legendary golden sword. Dashing through tangled vines she heard something. *Roar!* A man-eating tiger was cunningly prowling behind her! Suddenly she jumped in fright, she swiftly clambered under the emerald vines. Unsurprisingly, the furious tiger slashed straight through them. Finding herself by a beautiful, gushing waterfall, she realised that the golden, ruby encrusted sword was behind the waterfall. *Roar!* The deadly tiger was behind her, guarding the enchanted sword …

Chloe Garratt (10)
Glebefields Primary School, Tipton

THE MAJESTIC DAYDREAM!

Sprinting speedily, Mazie raced down the brown stairs. She tripped over a pair of ancient furry slippers! Amazingly, the next she knew, she somehow arrived into a mythical daydream. Though she was now stuck in the middle of a gushing waterfall, she desperately crawled out of the riverbank! Anxiously, she heard a twig crack! What was it? Gradually, the spiky bush shook briskly. Without warning she zoomed off despite something following her. Unfortunately, she bumped into a jagged palm tree!

Tegan Handley
Glebefields Primary School, Tipton

JUNGLE

All of a sudden, Carly accidentally trudged onto the filthy, muddy mud. Eventually Carly shouted, 'Anybody here?' Unfortunately nobody replied! Anxiously, she ran on. Amazingly, she splashed straight into a massive puddle! All the way up to her sensitive skin, she was fuming! She sprinted straight on to the slipperiest bridge. However, Carly had always been so terrified of the gushing waterfall. She slipped, she'd fallen straight into it. Surprisingly she didn't come back up …

Elle Dangerfield (10)
Glebefields Primary School, Tipton

RYAN'S ADVENTURE

Nervously Ryan was trying to shoot the tiger with a bladed, sharp dart. *Bang!* It missed. Sprinting rapidly through the damp jagged leaves, the tiger's fangs were razor-sharp, it was vicious, moreover deadly. Frantically, as he ran through the sluggy swamps the water splashed up his muscular arms. Cheering, Ryan was delighted until there was a huge, gigantic scream. All of a sudden the rocks started crumbling heavily into the sparkly stream. He was dangling by one hand …

Kallum Hyde (10)
Glebefields Primary School, Tipton

7

JUNGLE RUSH

Before long, explorer Dillen, slowly crept up to a vicious tiger that was as orange as the blazing sun. Animatedly, he shook slowly just in case, the savage tiger work up!

After a while he went on to explore and took loads of photos of birds, trees and many more. Even though it was a jungle and there were many surprises, he was not bothered. He went on a walk through the jungle and found a waterfall! What happened then?

Lily Johnson (10)
Glebefields Primary School, Tipton

THE GREAT CHASE

Because Charlotte was an excellent explorer, she had visited many brilliant places. Delighted, she triumphantly strode through the gracefully swaying palm trees. Abruptly, she heard a deafening roar! Her first thought was to swiftly clamber under the tough, snake-like vines.

Eventually the alarming tiger aggressively scratched through the tangled vines! She managed to slyly sneak away. Sprinting frantically, she wasn't concentrating where she was heading! Skidding, she came face to face with …

Aimee Holl
Glebefields Primary School, Tipton

THE GREAT CHASE

Gradually as the illuminate sun leisurely rose, Ross was strolling courageously across the rocky floor, he was seeking a miniscule tiger cub that was injured, so he could heal it. As he went to heal it the aggressive adult tiger viciously pounced out of nowhere! He rapidly sprinted away from the tiger. Unfortunately he reached the edge of the titan waterfall, the only choice he had was to leap onto the auburn green prolonged vines …

Ben Selwood (10)
Glebefields Primary School, Tipton

JUNGLE CHASE

Before long John, who was an explorer, was in the boiling jungle. Surprisingly, John saw an eerie orange tiger lying in his gigantic lair! He got closer and took a brilliant photo! The camera brightly flashed in the tiger's eyes. John walked away, the tiger slowly crept up on him and pounced! John ran as fast as he could, he ran past the old, rusty leaves. Then he went past the massive oak tree. After he fell in the river …

Tori Garratt (10)
Glebefields Primary School, Tipton

A STRANDED SOLDIER

Crawling schemingly through the decrepit, swampy path in the spine-chilling jungle, Slater heard a booming eerie noise. It was a gun! All of a sudden he sprinted rapidly through the grubby puddles as they splashed on his muscular arms, his heart pounded.
As time passed he trudged cautiously through the damp jagged leaves, he needed to get to the evacuation point. The gigantic mud paths opened out by him. Finally he made it! He raised his arms, however …

Jack Griffiths
Glebefields Primary School, Tipton

WHISKERS' JOURNEY BACK HOME

Whiskers had been at the zoo all his life, when it came to the day he had to be released. He tiptoed cautiously into the decrepit crate.
A little while after, the cold, cramped crate immediately stopped and the front shot off. Even though he didn't know where he was almost immediately he shyly crept onto the emerald, moist grass, in the distance a flowing, gushing waterfall majestically flew down a crumbling rock. Before very long, nothing was heard …

Lara Morris (11)
Glebefields Primary School, Tipton

TIGER CHASE

Confidently Treasure, also known as T, defiantly strode into the emerald jungle. She saw it, the auburn tiger cubs, with their mother. Treasure raised her arms protectively. She crept gradually towards them, the aggressive tiger mother was ready to pounce! Treasure's first thought was *run!* Courageously she sprinted away, her binoculars clanged against her athletic chest. She skidded to an abrupt halt as a sapphire waterfall appeared under her feet. Her safety was more important so she cautiously leaped …

Mara Harris (11)
Glebefields Primary School, Tipton

KATIE AND THE SPIDER MONKEY

Gradually, Katie, who had a colossal grin on her face, clambered treacherously through the jungle. The next moment, Katie heard a violent noise, *bang!* Yet bravely she carried on clambering down the glimmering path!
All of a sudden, a spider monkey surprisingly jumped out on her. It furiously screamed, 'Hua, hua!' She sprinted as fast as she could. She went through the gigantic palm tree, she carried on creeping then she painfully fell over a huge log. She quickly got up …

Charley Bowen (11)
Glebefields Primary School, Tipton

UNTITLED

Inconspicuously, the vicious tiger hid in the overgrown grass, ready to pounce on the timid man in his emerald Land Rover … Foolishly the tiger pounced, not knowing that the Land Rover's window was closed. Then *bang!* The tiger knocked himself unconscious. Luckily for the tiger the timid man, named Jim, was a vet so he helped the sly tiger up. The next moment, the confused Bengal tiger awkwardly staggered off into the Amazon rainforest.

Joel Mullett (10)
Glebefields Primary School, Tipton

UNTITLED

Very surprisingly, I caught a humongous, thunderous-tempered Bengal tiger. As time went by a hissing heroic sound bellowed from Cathy the luminous cobra. Consequently, Cathy fell off the tropical dazzling coloured tree. Something appeared behind her, it was a striped Bengal tiger. Cathy looked up, noticed and slithered away.

Meanwhile she slithered away up the enormous tree and noticed a small patterned parrot who was holding some roses that were completely multicoloured, holding them in his beak. He growled …

Cassia Roberts (10)
Glebefields Primary School, Tipton

SCARLET AND THE ALMIGHTY LION

Scarlet was being chased by an immense lion. She ran up a solid untamed tree. All of a sudden she fell down with an almighty clatter, straight into the almighty lion's mouth. She gave an almighty scream. 'Help me please …!'

Paige Lloyd (11)
Glebefields Primary School, Tipton

UNTITLED

With cat-like reflexes a humongous gorilla who had a wicked temper chased Bob through a wild treacherous jungle. Bob nervously climbed up the slimy tree but he swiftly slipped … The gorilla was intensely banging his chest, climbing up too. He grabbed hold of his ankle firmly.

Meanwhile, a tiger scratched the gorilla's leg with sharp claws. The gorilla dropped down off the tree rapidly and saw a mini tiger hunting for food. So the tiger gobbled up the gorilla.

Hayden Fox (9)
Glebefields Primary School, Tipton

ELLIE'S ESCAPE

Unfortunately, Ellie found herself being chased by a seven meter dart frog. She was extremely petrified, however astonished. Courageously, Ellie pulled a vine off an aged, untamed, tropical tree! Consequently, the tree fell down, but missed the evil frog! However, a radiant, vibrant, parrot swooped down gracefully and lifted the thin, towering vine out of Ellie's slender hand! Therefore that meant she had nothing to defend herself with! What will happen to Ellie? Will she save herself forever?

Elspeth McCann (10)
Glebefields Primary School, Tipton

CHLOE AND THE MYSTERIOUS WATERFALL

Briskly Chloe, who was adventurously trudging through the unique jungle, could hear a mysterious whispering behind her! Although Chloe was a bashful child, she was extremely determined to find out what that heroic sound was. Ultimately, Chloe thought she had found it, as she leisurely swiped the bushes away there it was, a remarkable, obscure waterfall! Mysteriously, Chloe found the waterfall but could now see shadows in the waterfall! Who was it behind there? Chloe's head was racing with questions.

Katie Hyde (10)
Glebefields Primary School, Tipton

THE CHASE

With cat-like reflexes, a petrifying, stripy and large Bengal tiger chased Leon through the haunted jungle! Leon was getting chased by a tiger, consequently he could die. Leon was muscular yet miniscule so he could hide in little places.

All of a sudden Leon climbed up the treacherous palm tree but the colossal tiger climbed up too. Suddenly, Leon swung on a delicate vine and crashed …

Connor Weaver (10)
Glebefields Primary School, Tipton

THE JUNGLE MONKEY

Although Jim had a four-wheel drive, he never thought that he would get stuck in a jungle … furthermore, a chocolate-brown monkey came leaping through the treacherous trees. Strangely he bellowed, 'Would you like a banana?'

'Yes please,' whispered Jim.

After that Jim got back into the maroon jeep, however he tried to get out of the mud.

At that moment the brown monkey came and pushed Jim into the spectacular waterfall …

Sam Hill (10)
Glebefields Primary School, Tipton

THE TORMENTED

Halley lived on her own, she was left when she was four, she was nine. However, she had black hair, cat-green eyes, black shirt and a dark blue chequered skirt. Suddenly Halley heard an old woman's voice saying, 'Halley, come here!'

Halley went, yet she closed her eyes and found herself in the Paris catacombs, tied to a chair. Simultaneously some weird creatures were tormenting her to find and give them a unicorn's heart, creatures, shadows and demons …

Marta Szczepanczyk (9)
Glebefields Primary School, Tipton

UNTITLED

In order of searching, John discovered a mystifying, irregular spider in a tropical tree. Although the spider was stripy, John intended on courageously climbing the colossal tropical tree, to find what he had been searching for. As John had climbed up the tree the spider had moved an inch. So John decided on carefully picking the spider up and taking it to his magnificent hut.

After a while, John found out he needed to name the spider Brazilian Phoneutria.

Sophie Prescott
Glebefields Primary School, Tipton

UNTITLED

George and Michael sat on a crooked branch playing about. George said, 'I'm hungry, can I have a bit of your banana please?'

'No,' said Michael, 'get one yourself.'

'No, no!'

Then Michael placed his banana on the branch. George said, 'Yum-yum.' He went to snatch it but then Michael smashed the banana out of his mouth by accident and made George fall. Then a big tiger was watching him with his red murderous eyes staring at George ...

Alisha May Elwell (10)
Glebefields Primary School, Tipton

GEORGINA AND JIMBOB

Aggressively, the immense gorilla grabbed the terrified, tranquil Jimbob by his bony, scrawny waist!

'Argh, let me go you fat gorilla!' Jimbob screamed.

'Hey, I'm not fat! And my name is Georgina!' Boldly, Georgina, the gorilla, roared once more, 'I only want to be friends!' she cried.

After that they became very close, they played with each other. Unfortunately Georgina died soon after they became close. That ruined Jimbob's life!

Ellie Smith (10)
Glebefields Primary School, Tipton

UNTITLED

Furiously, a vicious African lion grabbed a scavenging cheetah by his ribs. In retaliation the wounded cheetah insanely bit the wicked lion.

The next day that little horrible cheetah snuck up to the intelligent African lion and scratched the lion but it backfired on the demented cheetah because the lion powerfully scratched him on his belly. Panic-stricken, the cheetah sprinted away into the gigantic jungle and was never seen again.

Anthony Morgan (9)
Glebefields Primary School, Tipton

THE JUNGLE SAMBA

One rainy day there was a small cub, she had sparkling blue eyes and a red chequered nose with white dull dots spreading perfectness around her. She loved the jungle, every time she would wake in the early morning and race the purple beautiful birds flying high in the sky. Her mum didn't know what to call her but she did have an idea. The small cub and her mother were talking under the bamboo tree. She hoped she liked it.

Caitlin Bradnick (9)
Glebefields Primary School, Tipton

JUNGLE GIRL

One day in the jungle of Costa Rica, there was a pretty, strong girl called Zulu. Someone else was in the jungle … but was it something else? It was a fierce hunter looking for life which he wanted to check for human DNA. Carefully, the hunter lay down a trap to catch a human, but would he catch Zulu? It would be a close thing to call, crafty Zulu or fierce hunter?

William Jonathan White (9)
Glebefields Primary School, Tipton

IN THE LIGHT JUNGLE

In the adventurous terrifying jungle Sam Storm came to chop the leaves in his football strip. He is brave and loves football! It took all night to chop with his pocket knife and a torch but suddenly Sam Storm saw the lucky light to the treasure. He made his way to the treasure but had to cross a mountain so he put his walking boots and his hand claws and started to slowly climb, sweating but unfortunately he fell down …

Jack McGee (9)
Glebefields Primary School, Tipton

THE JUNGLE

In the Costa Rican jungle there was a boy called Jonathan Williams, he was swinging through the tropical trees in his camouflaged suit, when he spotted something terrifying. He ran for his life. Jonathan saw his opportunity to get away. He saw the island across the river. He ran across the slippy stones, leading to the island on the far side of the river. Stumbling, Jonathan splashed into the river but was taken away by thundering waterfall.

Ryan Cox (9)
Glebefields Primary School, Tipton

007

007 is in the big jungle. He spots a tiger and it chases after him. 007 runs and hides so the tiger can't find him. The tiger walks off searching for 007. He carries on with his adventure. 007 suddenly came to quicksand, 007 quietly climbed up a tree to avoid it. When he was up there he could see lots of wild animals – he needed to get out. Across the distance he saw a huge rock to climb …

Alex Tyler (9)
Glebefields Primary School, Tipton

UNTITLED

The cheeky little baboon that was called Sadie Jones, was swinging on the oak tree. All her friends were talking to her but she ignored them arrogantly. Then she was swinging on the enormous palm trees, then she climbed the tall mountain with her heavy walking boots. She had an ache so rested on a lion. She was so scared she sprinted like a cheetah. Then she was exploring for bananas but someone ate them all!

Chardinay Simkin (9)
Glebefields Primary School, Tipton

EXPLORING THE JUNGLE

Excitedly Mr M set off to the wild jungle. Mr M was lonely, arrogant and terrified because there were deadly creatures around the jungle. In a way, Mr M was excited because it was an experience, he had never been to a jungle before. Mr M's equipment was a camouflage coat, walking boots, knife, camouflage jeans and an army hat.
After a while Mr M sat down and ate his dinner. Suddenly a tiger sneaked up and bit him!

Ethan Plant
Glebefields Primary School, Tipton

THE JUNGLE BOY

Jungle Boy goes to the jungle jogging along the enormous trees and I see a lion walking around, Calmly I walk around the jungle silently, I see water and in there is a monkey and its name is Sneaky Jack. He loves to push people in soggy water and Sneaky Jack got pushed in. We were creeping along the big trees and we saw a tiger and when we reached the top, we could see all the views at the top.

Benjamin Kavanagh (9)
Glebefields Primary School, Tipton

UNTITLED

The little girl was exploring the sparkling waterfall. Suddenly the waterfall sparkled very bright then the little girl fell off the waterfall. But the little girl fell on a foggy tree. Then the tree whipped her so she got out her pocket knife and chopped the fruit off the trees. The girl set up camp on the tree.
The next morning the girl carried on with her journey.

Ashley Ralph (9)
Glebefields Primary School, Tipton

LOST IN THE JUNGLE

Content Jill, who was a psycho, took his energetic off-road vehicle on a cunning adventure to the wild! His colossal tank of fuel had run out! 'What a stroke of luck,' Jill muttered. He had made it to his destination. He saw a glamorous waterfall. A monkey turned up. He swung a banana to hit his vehicle with. The monkey, who was nude, pushed Jill into the crystal-clear waterfall. Jill was amazed with the magnificent Amazon waterfall.

Kyle Mason (9)
Glebefields Primary School, Tipton

ICY AND COLD, IT'S MOUNT EVEREST

I was there in Nepal, when suddenly there it was, it was Mount Everest. I stared with delight. I couldn't believe my eyes, now was my chance to get to the top. I started climbing in the freezing, frosty weather. I took one step, I could feel the snow whooshing in my face. I couldn't bear it any longer but I kept climbing. I reached the top. I saw an air balloon, it came to me and carried me down.

Angelena Randhawa (9)
Goldthorn Park Primary School, Wolverhampton

THE CLOUD BLEW OFF

Standing on top of a huge hill, staring at the beautiful, pleasant scenery that spread below me felt amazing. The weather was fantastic. Suddenly, the wind turned strong and pulled me up in the sky, jumping around on the clouds, no way! It wasn't that cold up here, probably as cold as a bench left outside in the winter. I slipped, tumbling down a hundred foot hill; will the clouds save me? The clouds were my final hope, I needed them ...

Shubham Dave (9)
Goldthorn Park Primary School, Wolverhampton

THE DREADFUL FLIGHT

It was my first flight after months of vigorous training, passengers had started to board the flight. I was to fly them over the sky-blue oceans to Iceland. I took off with precaution.
Before I knew it, I was halfway down the Norwegian Sea. The illumination of the dashboard light, which indicated engine failure, lit up. Suddenly, I could feel the plane losing altitude as we got closer to the icy blue sea, a tremble ... then, I woke up!

Indervir Dehal (11)
Goldthorn Park Primary School, Wolverhampton

EGYPT OR NONE?

As I walked across the gleaming hot sand, Johanna and I opened the pyramid of Tutankhamun. I was amazed to be in a pharaoh's tomb.

Afterwards I walked forward and surprisingly I found a thick blanket of gold. I was utterly shocked with aw and fear. Johanna and I were going to live in great luxury. As I continued along the mysterious corridor, I saw the coffin of Tutankhamun, it was so scary, scarier than an evil vampire. So terrifying!

Aashir Zaheer (10)
Goldthorn Park Primary School, Wolverhampton

AN ADVENTURE IN AGRA

Agra is a busy place. The Taj Mahal is situated in Agra. Today I have come by aeroplane to visit the Taj Mahal and to pray to God. I am tired and I can't walk any further, so I ride an elephant through the busy, crowded bazaar. I see lots of people bustling around in the markets. I see the sun shimmering on the Taj Mahal. I enter this beautiful place and I can't believe my eyes.

Neha Kainth (9)
Goldthorn Park Primary School, Wolverhampton

MY EXPEDITION TO ICELAND

Finally I succeeded, I had reached Iceland. All of a sudden sparkling snowflakes began to get heavier. I knew a blizzard was approaching. Would I survive? After a second I came up with a brilliant idea, which was to build an igloo to stay in. I had a terrible night, I could hear lots of noises and it was extremely cold. *Boom!* I was woken up by a loud noise. I realised it was only a dream. Phew, I'm safe!

Manisha Kalsi (11)
Goldthorn Park Primary School, Wolverhampton

THE MYSTERIOUS ISLAND AND THE BOOMING MONSTER

Boom! Boom! The trees shook from side to side. I was running as fast as I could, although I could hear the footsteps getting closer to me. Scared, nervous and tired, I managed to hide behind the bush. I could smell a revolting thing coming out of the bush. It was the monster. Suddenly he disappeared! I rubbed my eyes, and there it was, the mysterious island! I saw a shine so I ran to it. I slipped. 'Argh! Help!'

Kayleigh Hartill (11)
Goldthorn Park Primary School, Wolverhampton

THE TAJ MAHAL

The Taj Mahal is considered one of the 'Seven Wonders of the World'. The most precious part of this multi-marble monument is the tomb of Mumtaz Mahal which was built with white marble. She was the wife of the Emperor Shah Jahan. Agra is the place this beautiful monument can be found. In front of this wonder is a crystal-clear, blue river that flows in the middle of emerald-green trees.

Go and visit this beautiful, majestic monument.

Jaspriya Dhaliwal (9)
Goldthorn Park Primary School, Wolverhampton

THE KRAKEN APPEARS

Captain Starsight studied the map, a grim look appearing on his face, his galleon was entering the Bermuda Triangle. There came yells from outside his cabin as a large leathery tentacle smashed against the door, it gave way. Coiling around his waist, the tentacle pulled him from his cabin. A shot rang out and a bullet pierced its skin as the tentacle withdrew. A giant squid pulled itself out of the water, pushing the ship down into the icy sea.

George Taylor (10)
Goldthorn Park Primary School, Wolverhampton

MY JOURNEY TO THE GREAT WALL OF CHINA

I was walking along the Great Wall of China. My legs were hurting so I took a five minute break and sat down to rest them. I looked down. There was a magnificent view. I had nearly reached the end, my goal was about to be achieved. At the end I was feeling totally elated and proud of myself. I couldn't believe I had walked along the whole of the wonderful, tiring Great Wall of China! Amazing!

Alisha Kalsi (9)
Goldthorn Park Primary School, Wolverhampton

THE TAJ MAHAL

Long ago Shah Jahan was strolling down the Meena bazaar. He caught a glimpse of a young girl hawking silk and glass beads. After seeing the girl, Shah went to his father and declared he'd marry her. The two finally found love and married. Shah had turned Emperor and gave his wife the name Mumtaz Mahal. Meanwhile, when Mumtaz gave birth to their fourteenth child, she died. Shah promised her he would make her the most expensive deathbed.

Karina Lear (10)
Goldthorn Park Primary School, Wolverhampton

MY EXPERIENCE OF THE NORTHERN LIGHTS IN ICELAND

I was with my family and we were walking down the long, dark, snowy street. The air was cold and the sky was clear. Then suddenly there was a big flash of colour in the sky, It was beautiful and it looked as if millions of colours were dancing in the pitch-black night sky. It felt as if I was in Heaven and all the angels were above me. It was a once in a lifetime amazing experience.

Sonique Matharu (9)
Goldthorn Park Primary School, Wolverhampton

THE MIRACLE

It was freezing and the gusty winds were pulling me down the slippery surface. I was being tortured in the middle of a colossal storm. I powered my way through the enormous amount of snow that was surrounding me. Pain and agony swept through my body but I was determined to achieve this. I fought my way through the strong, powerful winds until I saw a jagged point. I smiled. I had finally reached the summit of Mount Everest.

Maninder Kallay (9)
Goldthorn Park Primary School, Wolverhampton

THE JUMP OFF THE BURJ KHALIFA!

I picked up the post with excitement. Wow! I won the competition, I rubbed my eyes to check again. I entered a competition to parachute jump off the tallest building in the world, the Burj Khalifa which was in Dubai. We arrived at Dubai and a limo took us to an amazing hotel.

The day of the jump, I was nervous and scared. Well, I couldn't jump so my dad, the superhero, jumped off instead.

Ariyan Patel (9)
Goldthorn Park Primary School, Wolverhampton

GRANDAD'S ABSURD FACT

During my recent trip to Grandad's village in India, Grandad warned me not to milk a cow as I would turn into one forever. After telling me what I thought was a ridiculous fact, I decided to put it to the test. I ran to the largest cow that my neighbours had in their stable and promptly milked it. Guess what? I didn't turn into a cow. This just goes to show that adults sometimes lie and make 'Moostakes!'

Gurleen Bhatti (10)
Goldthorn Park Primary School, Wolverhampton

JUST A DREAM IN INDIA!

Finally I've arrived in India! I hate that manky old plane that smells of stale cheese! The first thing I am going to do is eat something, as the meals on the plane are highly revolting. I struggle off and use a venue called 'Spice'. I order a piping hot Indian curry served with biryani. Suddenly, I hear a *crash* and *bang!* Then the ceiling breaks. Meteor falling on me! Noooo ... Phew ... it's just a dream! Yay for me!

Priya-Vidhya Patel (10)
Goldthorn Park Primary School, Wolverhampton

THE BIG CLIMB

I looked up, wondering how high this mountain was. I took a deep breath and with a groan I took a big push and climbed to the extreme! I managed to not stop, however it took most of my breath away.
After a few minutes I ran out of power and breath. I had no choice but to give up. I went down the mountain with ease. 'Well, that was a relief!' I gasped. 'Thank heavens, I didn't die!'

Akaam Shamerany (10)
Goldthorn Park Primary School, Wolverhampton

ZOMBIE GARAGE

One day the zombies were all hungry so they went to the town to eat some humans but there was nobody left. The zombies had to eat each other but the king of the zombies said, 'Don't eat people in other counties.'
They said, 'OK.'
However a little boy was hiding in the canal the boy found a knife and chopped them but the zombies came back so the zombies ate the boy and were full.

Gjok (9)
Hateley Heath Primary School, West Bromwich

NEVER-ENDING NIGHTMARE!

I was trapped in a murky box. I could hear chanting and it was moving. I tried to escape but I was frail. Suddenly the chanting stopped. Was I free? No! I was being dropped. It felt like forever. Never-ending! Quickly and helplessly, I pushed open the door but it didn't open. I was screaming and shouting but no one heard me. I was sweating like crazy. I then woke up thankfully, It was my nightmare!

Mustaf Rahman (10)
Hateley Heath Primary School, West Bromwich

THE SPECIAL DOOR

One day lived a girl named Poppy. Every time she went in the basement she felt very weird.

The next day she was tidying the basement and she found a door ... Poppy opened it and it was really bright. She saw lots of teddy bears and sweets, it was like she was in a dream. Suddenly the teddy bears started to talk and she made lots of friends. Every day she made cookies for them and played.

Ria Gharu (9)
Hateley Heath Primary School, West Bromwich

THE KING OF THE JUNGLE

There were once some animals but no king. Suddenly Gorilla said some people were attacking. Every animal thought the bravest animal who could stop them would be a king. First Giraffe tried, then Gorilla, then Elephant, then the rest. All the animals were too terrified and hid behind the tall enormous tree. Half of the animals' forest was chopped.

Soon a lion with courage roared ferociously and all of the people ran away. Lion was happy to be king.

Joey Li (9)
Hateley Heath Primary School, West Bromwich

33

AMAZING AFRICA

One day I was sitting in my room and I saw a sparkle in the tree out of my window. So I rushed downstairs then went outside. It was a magic, golden box. I opened it and *bam*, I was in Africa. Suddenly I got eaten by a lion.

A whole day went past, I was thinking of an idea. I got a feather and tickled him and he hurled me out. Suddenly I was in my room.

Priya Padwagga (9)
Hateley Heath Primary School, West Bromwich

THE LONELY LION

One day in a huge zoo lived a scary lion, he didn't have any friends at all because everyone thought he might eat them up. The lion wasn't a scary lion, he was a very friendly lion. The lion really wanted a best friend but everyone was so scared of him.

One day a new animal came to the zoo, her name was Emma and she became the lion's best friend and the lion was very happy that day.

Amanpreet Kaur (10)
Hateley Heath Primary School, West Bromwich

WATCH OUT!

At Christmas two boys were having a snowball fight. Then a plump man said, 'You want a ride?'

The boys got onto his red sleigh excitedly. They headed off to New York and flew over France in amazement. 'Our mum's are going to wonder where we are,' cried one of the boys.

'Don't worry,' said Santa, 'they're probably snoring their heads off.'

Suddenly one of the reindeer fell asleep and they bumped into an aeroplane. Were they dead …?

Jacob Peterkin (8) & Rizwan Mahmood (9)
Hateley Heath Primary School, West Bromwich

ENDING UP IN TUNISIA

We said goodbye to our parents and suddenly a pink fluffy sleigh appeared in sight. We flew over America and saw the Statue of Liberty! Cerys led the sleigh to Turkey and said, 'Look at the pools!' Then we flew over Ireland. Elise loved that lamb stew! The reindeer dropped us off in Tunisia, we didn't even know where we were but we loved it (very much!) All we could see was romance and people swimming in the sparkly pool!

Elise Harrison (8) & Cerys McDermott (9)
Hateley Heath Primary School, West Bromwich

SANTA'S CRAZY DAY

One 24th December tom was travelling across China, he found Santa's sleigh, he couldn't believe it!
Later that night he went back to the sleigh. 'Hello, do you want to go on the sleigh?' asked Santa.
They went over the Statue of Liberty and landed at the North Pole. Tom went to Santa's factory where the elves were making toys, they made amazing toys! The elves made good jokes too, it was so hilarious he could not breathe!

Arjun Gogna & Kieran Graham (8)
Hateley Heath Primary School, West Bromwich

STRANDED IN THE SNOW!

Harry wanted to find out how Santa delivered presents, so he went to an elf's workshop. 'Would you like to have a ride?' asked Santa.
'Yes please!' whispered Harry.
They jumped onto Santa's sleigh but immediately swooped past Japan and came to India. 'Wow!' Look at those houses. The Tower of London! My gosh! The Leaning Tower of Pisa!'
Suddenly Santa's pants fell down, Santa screamed! He was so embarrassed he flew off and left Harry stranded in the snow!

Priya Dhillon (9)
Hateley Heath Primary School, West Bromwich

HELPING SANTA

'Hello Santa!' shouted Mark.

'Hello Mark, join me around the world,' said Santa.

'Sure,' said Mark. So he hopped on. 'Wow!' gasped Mark, 'we're zooming past Antarctica, where are we going?'

'Africa,' Santa suggested.

They were dropping presents into houses in England, America, Africa and Italy. In Italy the Leaning Tower of Pisa was dancing. 'Have a safe trip home,' said Santa.

Mark arrived back in Antarctica and went home with his presents. He went to bed and slept.

Arif Rhaman & Ben Humphries (8)
Hateley Heath Primary School, West Bromwich

THE BRILLIANT CHRISTMAS EVE

I was in Antarctica then Santa said, 'You can go on my sleigh if you want to?'

'Always,' said Tom.

Tom sat on Santa's sleigh and went off in the air. 'Look there's the Himalayas and the Golden Temple,' shouted Tom.

'There are the pyramids, the Great Wall of China,' replied Santa.

'And the Liberty Statue!' cried Tom excitedly.

Suddenly Santa's gear went out and they crashed into the Leaning Tower of Pisa, tragically. Were they dead?

Gurpreet Singh (8)
Hateley Heath Primary School, West Bromwich

AROUND THE WORLD IN ONE NIGHT

'Hi Danny,' the boy said, 'there's you present Danny!' he said.

Danny looked outside, a sleigh like Santa's. 'This is for me?' he cried. The sleigh flew to China, New York, North Pole, Brazil and France, all over the world. Danny felt really tired, putting all the presents they wished for down the chimney. They flew home and went to sleep.

Suddenly Danny heard a noise. 'Get up Danny, it's Christmas!'

Was it true or just a dream?

Lanz Masangkay (9)
Hateley Heath Primary School, West Bromwich

CONNOR'S TRIP WITH SANTA

Santa came to my house from Lapland. I crawled into his sleigh. He took me all around the world. I peered over Santa's sleigh and then Santa said, 'No need to be scared, look there's China, Turkey and England.' I went back home and Santa brought me a present. The next day I was in my bed. I opened my present. Was that a dream last night?

Connor-Jon Smith (9)
Hateley Heath Primary School, West Bromwich

ALASKA TROUBLE

Tom, Ben and Sarah were trudging through the cold snow. Suddenly they found a husky with a lamp. They took the husky and the lamp to their house. Sarah thought that someone abandoned the husky. After, Tom heard Sarah talking loudly, he wished that she'd be quiet and then Sarah couldn't talk again. Tom ran to Sarah and said he was sorry. He ran to the genie to ask him to redo the wish. He said, 'I can't.'

Sana Malik (11)
Hateley Heath Primary School, West Bromwich

THE AMERICAN DISASTER

Suddenly a bomb blew up the Bank of England! A robber called James and his girlfriend Tulisa, now needed six hundred thousand pounds to escape from England to America, so they could clear the country of vampires and zombies. Tulisa knew a guy with sixty weapons in his shop.

When they got to America they got the weapons. They fought for days on end. It took a week. There were two creatures left, one bullet. James shot, both died!

Daniel Coley (11)
Hateley Heath Primary School, West Bromwich

THE ONE REMAINING BOY

Bang! 'The engine has blown. What are we going to do? We're heading towards a mountain,' shouted Ryan.

'Argh!' everyone shouted and screamed until their voices disappeared.

Suddenly *crash!* The plane disappeared and left a cloud of smoke and fire which suddenly faded away. Only one person fell to the ground. What happened to the other two? Then he found himself in a cage. He saw a star and made a wish to be back home …

'I'm home!' said Ryan.

Lyndan Hohn (11)
Hateley Heath Primary School, West Bromwich

TOP OF THE WORLD

He was the first man to climb a mountain called Chomolungma. Chomolungma is one of the biggest mountains in the world. The day he climbed the mountain he had to go back down because there was a big storm. When he got back he had to go to the hospital, he was very ill but he did not give up on his dream.

Eventually he climbed the mountain again and reached the top successfully. He is a very brave strong man!

Molly Evans (9)
Hateley Heath Primary School, West Bromwich

A CHRISTMAS MIRACLE

Bang! Sarah dropped her present, it was nearly Christmas. She couldn't wait. Sarah was going to see Santa today. Then she heard a voice that she had never heard before. 'Christmas is boring, why do you like Christmas? You make my life miserable,' something shouted.
'Who said that?' she shouted back.
'I'm the Christmas tree and you're not going to have a good Christmas, you're trapped!'
She saw the star's head and made a wish.
'Merry Christmas,' the tree said.

Selina Malhi (11)
Hateley Heath Primary School, West Bromwich

MYSTERIOUS MAN

Long ago there lived a mysterious man who would never show his identity. To me he was just a stunt man because I always see him do mind-blowing stunts, such as jumping out of a plane with no parachute. Crazy! I wonder who taught him those. I was on my way home and a man jumped out of a plane and landed outside my house. But hey, it was the guy I saw on TV!

Harry Chander (11)
Hateley Heath Primary School, West Bromwich

THE HAUNTED HOUSE

There was a family going to live in the haunted house. They came from a different country so they didn't know if it was haunted. The family walked in the house. 'This house needs a clean!' *Slam!* The door went.

'Ha, ha ha, you are my slaves now. First thing is to tidy the house up. It will take a week.'

They tidied the house. 'I've had enough!' the dad smashed the window. They ran out. What a week!

Jusleen Dulay (10)
Hateley Heath Primary School, West Bromwich

THE NAUGHTY GENIE!

It was a horrible snow day. The houses were covered with snow. A loud bang, everyone could hear. Katie went to look outside but nothing was there. Something called her name. She looked behind but nothing waited. A genie popped out and said, 'Have one wish only for finding me.'

Katie took her wish which was to have a dog. She got the dog. It was magical. *Bang!* The genie disappeared. Life would never be the same for her!

Baljit Kaur (11)
Hateley Heath Primary School, West Bromwich

BIG BEN

'Wow!' shouted Bob. He was shocked at the thought of seeing the colossal clock. He wanted to stay in a hotel where he could see the massive clock through his bedroom window all day and all night. He was amazed at the sight of Big Ben. 'One billion people come here every day I bet,' Bob said, staring in amazement.

All day Bob just sat in London on a bench staring at the clock, dreaming about how amazing it is …

Umar Salim (10)
Holy Trinity CE Primary School, Handsworth

SAFE

On a cold winter's day I went to the mosque. On the way I met a bloke and he asked me, 'Where are you going?'

I said, 'To the mosque.'

He said, 'I'll take you.'

I said, 'OK.'

He took me to the church. I said, 'I am not a Christian, I'm a Muslim.'

He tried to grab me into the church. I quickly ran … I reached the mosque. I entered and I felt the warmth and love inside.

Sunah Iqbal (10)
Holy Trinity CE Primary School, Handsworth

THE BIG BEN, LONDON TOWER

I entered. I saw the beautiful place. I was right in front of the Big Ben clock. My experiences changed. I saw the gold, I just wanted it! I was amazed, it was really tall. I dreamed that one day it was dead. The London Tower, Big Ben! I wanted to stay in front of it and stare at it. My imagination changed. Finally I was thinking of all the things I could do with gold. My last chance to explore.

Summayha Zaman (10)
Holy Trinity CE Primary School, Handsworth

THE BIG MISTAKE OF MY LIFE!

There I was in the middle of the desert. No way, should I go north, south, east, west? I was at the centre of the world. Words rushed through my mind. What should I do? Suddenly I heard a rumble underneath, it was crawling and forming into a tornado! Running as fast as I could I fell into a pit a hundred miles down. How did I get into this big unexpected mess? What should I do? My solution was: 'Help!'

Folasayo Kayode (11)
Holy Trinity CE Primary School, Handsworth

THE TEMPLE OF SPARTA

Hercules had a dream about the Temple of Sparta, he knew he had to conquer his fear of the witch but he had to go and do his chores.

He had his breakfast, after he went to the armour shop. Hercules had loads of armour. Hercules was on his way to the temple. He opened the gate and he saw the witch. Hercules ran to him and stabbed him in the heart. He took the witch's saw. Everyone was freed.

Stephan Thompson (10)
Holy Trinity CE Primary School, Handsworth

THE BEST BIRTHDAY PRESENT

Sarah's birthday was coming up so she asked her mum if they could go to London for a special birthday present. 'Of course we can!' said Mum, hoping she could go on a shopping spree for new things.

A week passed, when Sarah woke up and got ready. She had many birthday gifts. 'Now for the last present, we are going to London, all of our things are packed so let's go, go, go to London,' said my lovely mum.

Tahirah Brou-Martin (11)
Holy Trinity CE Primary School, Handsworth

UNTITLED

My heart was racing, faster than Usain Bolt. My cheeks were glowing green, ready to get sick! I had just reached the top of the Eye. My legs wobbled like jelly, ready to be eaten. I was sweating or more like raining! I sat down in confusion, who would dig my grave? My mum or my dad? It moved, my luck had finally come until it stopped again. I thought, *I'll never lose a bet again*.

David Johnson (11)
Holy Trinity CE Primary School, Handsworth

LOST IN NEW YORK

As I rushed to the church I fell and bust open my lip. Normally I would have gone home, but as I was lost in New York I had no hope of finding my way home whatsoever. *Boof!* 'Oh!' As I smashed the doors open I hit my head.

I then scrambled through the first aid box. I then found a poisonous blade. Then I ran tripping up on a bench. Opening the door I found a spooky graveyard …

D'André De Costa (10)
Holy Trinity CE Primary School, Handsworth

OUT OF BREATH

I ran with all my power, I never looked back. My heart was throbbing. I reached the mall. I was out of breath. I stood as still as a statue. I saw the police go by so I walked like any other person.

So let me tell you why I was running. I was on the train and the ticket man came but I had no cash on me so I pulled the emergency brakes and ran …

Nikira Parris (10)
Holy Trinity CE Primary School, Handsworth

WHY ME?

I woke up to the starry night as it glistened. My baby sister woke up to find me curled like a ball; my heart pumping, I could feel the bumps in my legs. Having flashbacks and vomiting; hearing helicopters, cars and alarms made me hallucinate. I saw black and as I clambered to the surface I saw a bottle that looked yellow and purple I took it and drank it in a gulp. I knew I had made a mistake.

Lasharnna McEwan (10)
Holy Trinity CE Primary School, Handsworth

THE BOGEY OF THE STATUE

I clambered into the lift. The city of New York was beautiful from above. As I raced into her head, the view from above was outstanding. As I leaned over the bars it happened; I fell. I was suspended in mid-air. I was like a giant bogey out of the Statue of Liberty. Ten harsh minutes later I was rescued from a breathtaking moment. The price was expensive but come on, wouldn't you have done it?

Gurveer Lally (10)
Holy Trinity CE Primary School, Handsworth

RUNAWAY!

I was running as fast as I could. I didn't know where I was or what I was doing. Some people were chasing me for money. I was out of breath, nowhere to go, sweating and scared of what they will do to me. Suddenly I heard a voice. 'Seize him!' I found a door by me, opened it and found myself standing by the Eiffel Tower. Suddenly a voice said, 'Welcome to Hell!'
I shrieked, 'Argh!' in terrible pain.

Adam Rahman (11)
Holy Trinity CE Primary School, Handsworth

BIG BELL

On a hot summer's day I went to London for a holiday. I didn't know who or where I was going, I was lost so I was just roaming from street to street. Then I got on a street that led me to the big Bell. It was the most beautiful thing I ever saw. Its colour was gleaming gold underneath the sun. That is where I went.

Leke Sokunbi (11)
Holy Trinity CE Primary School, Handsworth

THE TAJ MAHAL

The Taj Mahal is amazing and beautiful. It's made of pure marble. You'll get hot but also receive water. You'll get some interesting facts from guides. The queue line is amazingly long to get inside but the view is wonderful. Different cultures have been there and everyone seemed to be enjoying it! You can get pictures taken by photographers or you could bring your own camera, you'll also see a beautiful river flowing alongside you. You'll enjoy this trip!

Roma Banger (10)
Holy Trinity CE Primary School, Handsworth

MY FAVELA MAGIC TRICK

I was about to perform my magic trick in front of the Statue of Christ in Favela! I just started feeling dizzy as soon as I started to ascend from the ground, the audience watched me in amazement. I started to rise and the crowd was cheering. I felt like a celebrity. My feet were shaking constantly as I was ascending. The audience was cheering so much! I was like a mini structure of the Statue of Christ! Loved it!

Umair Razwan (10)
Holy Trinity CE Primary School, Handsworth

BABY JAKE

'Mamma?' said baby Jake.
'What is it?' said his mom.
Baby Jake just said, 'I wanna … '
'What?' said Mom,
Baby Jake couldn't speak that well.
Years went by and baby Jake was now eight. His mom asked him, 'When you were younger there was something you wanted.'
'I wanted to go to Jamaica because that's where Grandad lived.'
'Oh,' said his mom, 'you just had to ask.'

Richantae Campbell-Howell (9)
Holy Trinity CE Primary School, Handsworth

THE BOY AND HIS MOUSE

Long ago there lived the Anderson family. They had a son called Andy. Andy had a pet mouse called Pip. Andy loved him. He did not like to play at all. He didn't have any friends either. Andy made a wish. He wished that Pip could talk to him.

The next day something happened. Pip started to talk. Andy could not believe his eyes. Andy wanted to go away forever so he did. He said he would return later.

Maryam Mahroof (9)
Holy Trinity CE Primary School, Handsworth

THE SCHOOL REPORT

I had to do a school report. I had a dream while sleeping. I went to Spain, it was beautiful. I went to the beach, it was very relaxing. I went to Jamaica, I had some juicy fruit. I went to the circus, I went all over the world. *It is real,* I thought while writing my report on all the travelling I had been doing, discovering different countries, its cultures, people. Turns out it was all … a dream!

Desjanae Williamson (10)
Holy Trinity CE Primary School, Handsworth

TODAY

Today I was going to a doggy park, a very wonderful doggy park of course. I am a very cute cocker spaniel. I have reddy-orange patches and pure white coat. It's very soft and it gets washed 2 days a week, usually, Monday and Friday. I have big brown eyes that give me that cuteness, I've a wonderful diamond-studded pink collar, it's my favourite. I've got dozens of different collars like green, aqua, also blue, purple and gold.

Abigail Salt (10)
Leamore Primary School, Walsall

THE BEST DAY EVER

I went to America to celebrate my brother's birthday. We went to Disney World. We saw Mickey Mouse and Ben Ten, my brother's favourite. After that we went back to the hotel and we all went to sleep.
In the afternoon we had juicy strawberries with melted milk chocolate we saw Bruno Mars buying some cocoa, very unusual to see a celebrity!
I wish we all could go again very soon. It was a really great day. Happy birthday Billy.

Natalie Westley (10)
Leamore Primary School, Walsall

UNTITLED

The day I went to the Bermuda Triangle I went flying out my boat when I grabbed onto the corner of the boat. My boat got trashed and the minute after, I was on an island where there was a tree that could walk and talk! It was a coconut tree. The tree started to throw coconuts at me. I ran and ran as fast as I could. I stopped and looked. Nothing there.
'Argh!' It was a dream!

Jamie Lee Hendy (10)
Leamore Primary School, Walsall

UNTITLED

The day I was in New York. The yellow cabs zoomed past me as I stood staring at the Statue of Liberty. Big flash adverts flicked on and off the massive screens. I had never seen a town so busy in my life. Shop doors opened and closed as people walked out with big carriers bags on their hands. I walked into the gift shop and bought a yellow fridge magnet with New York on. It was really good.

Billie Whitehouse (10)
Leamore Primary School, Walsall

RAY GUN MADNESS

I pulled out my ray gun and pointed it at evil Dr Pork Chop but all of a sudden, *bang, boom!* People jumped into the building. They all pointed their guns at me! I was scared. Someone shot at me. I jumped out the way then another person shot at me. I jumped out of the way again. I pulled out my ray gun and shot them all dead.
I shouted, 'I did it, I did!'

Riley Tipton (10)
Leamore Primary School, Walsall

UNTITLED

I went on a cruise for one week with my whole family, even my nan, grandad, auntie, uncle, mom, dad, sister and brother. We had to put my cat in a kennels and my other cat with my next-door neighbour.
We went in a taxi and went to Birmingham airport. We met all my family there. We got on a plane and flew to Spain. There we got on a ship. Holiday!

Sophie Edmonds (10)
Leamore Primary School, Walsall

CHRISTMAS TIME

I ran downstairs to open my presents but they weren't there. I went upstairs to my mom. I said, 'Mom, where are my presents?'
'Well dear, it's Christmas tomorrow.'
'How? But it is the 24th!'
'Yes, so it's not Christmas because it is the 25th when it's Christmas.'
I ran downstairs and there were my big presents. I unravelled the paper off it. I'd forgotten Christmas was the 25th.

Levi Cox (10)
Leamore Primary School, Walsall

UNTITLED

I walked down the long road, I wanted an adventure I ran home and went down the basement. I got in the machine and I was there Jurassic park. I could smell horrible dinosaur mess. I found a tyrannosaurus and rode him through the spooky forest. Then with a *bang* I fell off the dinosaur down onto the ground and cut my knee. But I was OK. I lived in a little hut for the rest of my life.
'Argh!'

Elle Sandford (10)
Leamore Primary School, Walsall

THE TERRIFYING LEAP

The Italian chased me onto the roof of a flat. I saw him closing in on me. I was getting close to the edge I turned round and ran off the edge.

The next thing I knew, I was in mid-air, flying over the city, watching the city underneath.

We are in a traffic jam with car horns beeping. I didn't think I was gonna make it I stuck my arms up and grabbed the ledge.

It was game over.

Daniel Smith (10)
Leamore Primary School, Walsall

THE STRANGE CREATURE

I lay down on my bed not tired at all. I reached down underneath my bed and got out my favourite book. I got too engrossed all of a sudden there was a *crash* of thunder and a flash of light, then I got sucked into the book!

I wandered around and ran straight into something that looked like a bear with one eye and a walking stick. He took one look at me and ran away whimpering quietly …

Charlie-Ann Hammonds (10)
Leamore Primary School, Walsall

UNTITLED

I lay on my bed hearing my heart beating very fast. I turned and faced the door, the light turned on but nobody was there. I struggled and got out from my blanket. Then I opened the door, no one was there. I looked down; my mother's wedding ring was there. I picked it up then ran into Mum's room but she wasn't there. I went into my bedroom and put Mum's ring on my desk and then …

Candice Jones (10)
Leamore Primary School, Walsall

MONSTER MADNESS

One day I played outside with a hairy, ugly, tall monster with a big red nose. Then his mother cooked dinner, it was worms, glass, chicken. The drink was milk then Mr Post took the ugly monster with him.
After that Joy, the boy, (10-year-old) sobbed his eyes. The monster was angry, like a hippo. He had big red eyes and looked side to side for dinner. I waved bye then he disappeared.

Ben Thacker (10)
Leamore Primary School, Walsall

UNTITLED

I sprinted to Paris like a cheetah. I stopped, I felt very dizzy afterwards. I had my little break. I got back up and I felt as fit as a fiddle. I did a great challenge with Big Foot to climb up the Eiffel Tower. I went as quickly as I could.
When I made it I thought I was dying with tiredness
When I got back down I thought, *I will take the stairs next time!*

Lewis Morris (10)
Leamore Primary School, Walsall

CANDY LAND

I woke up in the middle of Candy Land. It was very weird. If you woke up in the middle of Candy Land would you be freaked out? I bit into a candy lollipop and it went *bang!* It scared me to death. I jumped out of my skin like a skeleton. All I could hear was 'Hello'. I picked up a candy lolly and bit it. I suddenly thought that I was in a nightmare!

Elle Wallbank
Leamore Primary School, Walsall

HOLIDAY DESTINATION: EGYPT

In a sandy land across the Nile there lived a family of five. They had three camels who were eating the herbs the children gave earlier and they had two bicycles. You could see outside an immense sandstorm, it was heading their way!

They shirked, 'Please don't tumble over our house!' Suddenly the storm magically turned into a sandy wind. They couldn't see a thing except the windy air. It was quite a whirly day and it was fun.

Sara Isse Ahmed (11) & Asim Muhammad (10)
Manor Park Primary School, Aston

A JOURNEY TO THE EIFFEL TOWER

'Mum, why can't I go to the Eiffel Tower?' asked Christina.

'Sorry, it's so risky and hazardous. You can't go. Now go to school,' said Mum.

Christina walked away in misery and it took several minutes for Christina to get into school.

As Christina walked leisurely back home she had a ludicrous thought, *I have a splendid idea. My mum is not here. She has to miss her interview with the ex-president.*

As she took her first step …

Ekoko Pese (10)
Manor Park Primary School, Aston

THE MYSTERIOUS EVILS TRIANGLE

In the western part of the Atlantic Ocean, there it was the triangle that everything vanished in! A group of travellers explored landmarks, investigating how people disappeared in the mysterious Bermuda.

Meanwhile the travellers then spotted a boat crossing by the triangle. Mr Brunnell rushed towards the mystical triangle looking to see if the boat was still there. He went underwater to investigate how the boat vanished. They all were hoping for him to come back and not disappear.

Shabana Rakhda (11)
Manor Park Primary School, Aston

MY LONG SPRINT TO THE AMERICAN ICE CREAM VAN

I sprinted, step by step, going up and down until I collapsed. It felt like I was sprinting for centuries. The creaks from the floor crackled. I believed I could make it but yes, yes, I heard the sweet musical sound from my destiny, an ice cream van.

Eventually I saw the light! It was yellow, brown and pink, all the colours of an ice cream. I could not believe it, I'd achieved my fate, there I was waiting … hooray!

Ameera Rehman (10)
Manor Park Primary School, Aston

THE GREAT GHOST SHIP OF RICHMOND VIRGINIA

One day in the murky streets there was howling. One person who was petrified was Helen, with arachnophobia. Her mother sent her to the old shop. She saw a shimmering metallic colour in the sky and in a flash she disappeared!

When she woke up she found a spider on her shoulder, she shrieked as loud as a banshee. She turned and found herself imprisoned by ghosts. One ghost laid his hands on Helen.

Helen said, 'Where am I?'

Midhat Choudhury (10) & Leesum Michael Kelly (11)
Manor Park Primary School, Aston

THE LOST TWINS

'I love the Eiffel Tower,' he said to his twin brother. He wanted to go up the Eiffel Tower so he walked to the bakers shop with twelve Euros so he could buy a croissant for his breakfast.

When he finished he made some wings out of leather to fly off the tower. He climbed up step by step. He exclaimed to his brother, 'Don't tell Mum!'

He told Mum but he jumped and sang, 'I believe I can fly!'

Nirobii Goffe (11)
Manor Park Primary School, Aston

THE NIAGARA FALLS TRAGEDY

There once lived a boy and girl in France. They didn't have any parents so they decided to be adopted. They lived in Canada with their new parents. They both ran away because their owners were very vain. They then lived in the Niagara Falls. The flow of the water dripping in their face felt wonderful but one day they used all the water up and there was a drought! Everybody suffered, nobody survived except the boy and the girl.

Samir Mohammed (11)
Manor Park Primary School, Aston

THE LOST BOY AND GIRL

Once there was a boy called Oliver and a girl called Shirell. They went to the bakery to purchase a loaf of bread. They chose garlic bread to have with their supper. They had twenty Euros left; they decided to buy some croissants to have for their breakfast.
Once they had bought their food they went back home, but Oliver dashed ahead at alarming speed. Shirell said, 'Where is my brother? Oliver, Oliver?' They were never seen again for life!

Mya Smith (10)
Manor Park Primary School, Aston

THE LIGHT

It all started with us on the beach. 'Over here, look at this!' So I turned around, positioned in front of a huge old ship. I stepped inside hearing funny and echoing voices. It was really dark, darker than the sky at night. Then there was a light; a light which I knew wanted me to follow. I followed it out of the ship. It lead me right out to the front of my doorstep. So here I am.

Shahnaz Begum (11)
Manor Park Primary School, Aston

STARLIGHT THE DOG

I once went to France to my cousin's house; she had a dog called Starlight. She was light brown and white. I liked Starlight because she did tricks like walking around on her back legs, jumping through hoops and rolling over. I told her too. Starlight was very entertaining. The dog did not make mess, she listened and she was a really interesting dog. That visit seeing Starlight, made me want to have my very own little dog too.

Miza Nsuenga (10)
Manor Park Primary School, Aston

THE EARTH'S SURFACE

I was walking on the Earth's surface; I thought I was going to fall through. My mind was confused and I didn't know what to do. I saw the dark sky and I could see lots of little stars. I was thinking about how I was going to get back to my house and then suddenly I fell through and screamed loudly as possible. I landed on the floor, my back was hurting and I'd dropped into a different country.

Amani Rahman (11)
Manor Park Primary School, Aston

MY JOURNEY IN A HOT AIR BALLOON

The view's captivating. I feel like a bird soaring through the sky. There's fire above me but I'm not scared I'm floating on air, weightless. Up here, I haven't a care in the world. I don't worry if I'm the right colour. People say I'm not, but being black is good up here, in the hot air balloon. It makes one stand out against the sky, not fade into the background. Whereas on Earth I wish I did.

Amy Legge (11)
Manor Way Primary School, Halesowen

THE POPPY

I'm a poppy looking for a friend. I've been in this box for days, maybe months. What's this? What's happening? I'm being pinned to something, it's dark blue and there is a pretty girl. It's bright and sunny and very cold, there is music and we start to move marching together in straight lines. All through the town we march, this is what I was made for, I'm so proud.

Grace Tristram (10)
Manor Way Primary School, Halesowen

THE TERRIFYING DELIGHT

Days I've waited, hours I've queued, longing yet fearing, but it was too late. We're here!
'Just one for Terror Tower?'
'Yes,' I gulped to the park assistant. It was too late to turn back now. Nervously, I sit waiting for the countdown.
Suddenly my heart was in my mouth. Flashing, whizzing, screaming, dropping, these emotions rushing through my head.
One minute later, it was over. Days I'd waited, hours I'd queued minutes it was over. What a terrifying delight!

Rebecca Parkin (10)
Manor Way Primary School, Halesowen

THE RACE OF LIFE

I ran and ran for what seemed like miles, it was still all the way up the road, I could make it. Rapidly, I twisted my head to see if they were gaining on me. They were! I tugged at my rucksack to pull it back on my shoulder. A hand shot out and grabbed my arm. The only thing I thought now was to rip it off and run. I did and I made it, home sweet home. Phew!

Cerese Li Lyon-Bailey (10)
Manor Way Primary School, Halesowen

TASTE OF VICTORY

I grinned so hard all of my glistening teeth could be seen. Music blared through the black speakers as I hummed nonchalantly to the beat. The suspense grew and eventually shattered as I showed my true colours. Finally, the only thing that I was good at could be shown at last – dancing. I was proud and happy. Knowing that I had dreamt of this moment forever made it more special. That's why it was my taste of victory.

Victoria Heath (10)
Manor Way Primary School, Halesowen

THE AMAZING JOURNEY

As I walk in the plane, the door shuts behind me. I get in my seat ready for lift off.

On the way I see the most amazing things like the massive Eiffel Tower, the Statue of Liberty, even Big Ben!

But the journey has ended and I think I'm better at home instead.

Daniel Lyndon (11)
Manor Way Primary School, Halesowen

THE STORMY MOUNTAIN

There was once a mountain. A boy decided to climb the mountain. He was climbing the mountain when he got halfway up suddenly it started to rain which made it very slippery. Also the mist was coming down. The boy was stone cold. But there was a problem, he slipped when there was a storm and fell down, but he didn't give up and stopped and climbed again. He got to see the top and slid down.

Todd Sasin (10)
Manor Way Primary School, Halesowen

THE MYSTERIOUS CHASE

Waiting, waiting, I'm scared as it's getting ready to attack. Nevertheless I can't be scared I have to think of a plan otherwise I'm meat ready to be killed. I run, run for my life. Though I don't dare look back, I can sense it getting nearer. I turn a corner but no! It is a dead end.

Suddenly something hits me in the back, it is a shopping trolley. A shopping trolley! Why am I so scared?

Cameron Davies (10)
Manor Way Primary School, Halesowen

MY SOUL TO TAKE

A terrifying tale of the Riverton Ripper, legend was he swore he'd return to murder the seven children born the night he died.

Sixteen years after people were disappearing. Had the Ripper returned to take revenge? Did he survive the night he was left for dead? Had he been reincarnated as one of the seven? Only one of the seven had the answers. If they hoped to save their friends they must face an evil that won't rest ever again!

Akena Clements (10)
Manor Way Primary School, Halesowen

UNTITLED

I'm a pair of shoes; I go on people's feet, every day I get worn. Mostly everyone calls me the looking pair. There was a competitor, a race. We started at the race line and then beep, the race had started. I ran as fast as I could, skipping and hopping along the track. I won, hooray! I was glad I won. Can you guess what I am?

Chloe Humphries (10)
Manor Way Primary School, Halesowen

SPACE HOPPING

Jim opened his eyes to find himself stranded in an alien world. 'Where are we?' he screamed.
'I don't know,' replied Ben.
Jim wandered about feeling stressed. Jim was getting hot. 'How come it's so hot?' he asked.
'Maybe it has something to do with the two suns up here?' Ben mumbled.
'I'll try repairing our spaceship.' The ship, a couple of metres away was in extremely bad shape.
An hour later the spaceship was ready to go home.

James Harcourt (10)
Manor Way Primary School, Halesowen

HOW THE CROCODILE GOT HIS BUMPY SCALES

In a dark jungle there lived a crocodile named Eddie. Unfortunately Eddie was not like the other crocodiles because Eddie had no bumpy scales. That's right, Eddie's back was as smooth as a pebble.

One day, in the middle of December, changes started to appear in the jungle. Small white flakes started drifting down from the sky. It grew so cold that Eddie formed goosebumps on his back. The weather stayed like this for ages and Eddie's scales never disappeared.

William Rowley (11)
Manor Way Primary School, Halesowen

THE HOLIDAY GHOST GIRL

One cold and mysterious night, Rachel was on holiday with her family, they were staying in a caravan. On that night Rachel heard a noise, she went out the caravan and followed the noise all the way to the beach. Then, in the sea, there was a ghost, standing in the water. She made Rachel drown in the sea to get revenge for when someone drowned her when she was on holiday. The ghost was never seen again.

Chloe Palmer (11)
Manor Way Primary School, Halesowen

A MASSIVE ACCIDENT – OR WAS IT?

I was sailing on the Bermuda Triangle; I'd almost reached the middle when I saw a dot in the sky. It seemed to be coming closer, so I looked through the telescope. It was so close I took it away and bang! The so-called 'dot' was actually a vast meteor which had crashed into my ship.

Now I am an old disabled lady, now I don't have any legs but a scarred face. Remember, beware of the Bermuda Triangle!

Isha Pooni (10)
Manor Way Primary School, Halesowen

A DAY IN THE COUNTRYSIDE

I rise up into the open in a clutched up space eating my picnic, seeing all the places I have never seen before. Children in the fields playing hide-and-seek, tag, I cannot believe my eyes, gardens looking pretty as ever. I see people driving to and from work in the rush hour. I think to myself, *this is the best day I have ever had in the countryside exploring and sightseeing the world itself.*

Ellie Field (10)
Manor Way Primary School, Halesowen

DOLPHINEAS

Under the picturesque seas lay the city, Atlantis. There was a radiant attractive dolphin maid called Dolphineas. Dolphineas had blonde silky hair with a very light black tip at the top.

On a stormy thunderous night, a Spitfire pilot was getting closer and closer to the shimmering water of the Atlantic. Then Sharkation came up and claimed one more victim. Suddenly, Dolphineas came up and got this razor-sharp blade out of her pocket and stabbed Sharkation saving the pilot.

Dylan Garbett (Tomlin) (11)
Moorcroft Wood Primary School, Bilston

VISITING SCOTLAND

'But Mum,' shouted Tory.
'I've already packed the car Tory and you are coming to Scotland with me!' shouted Mum.
Slowly Tory made her way to the car.
Finally they reached Aunt's house.
After lunch Tory went to bed.
It was 3am when Tory awoke to a noise and ran to the kitchen and grabbed a knife. Apprehensively she went to the garden and found the Loch Ness monster. She slashed Nessie.
Slowly she awoke from her dream.

Felicity Taylor (11)
Moorcroft Wood Primary School, Bilston

A DAY AT THE BEACH

Sunbathing in Tunisia, I sat by the pool and ate a strawberry-flavoured ice cream. It was a boiling hot day so my family and I decided to go to the beach and play some games.

Then my brother said, 'I'm going into the sea for a swim!'

So I replied, 'Be careful of the mermaids!'

Unfortunately he was never seen again. He must have fallen in love with a mermaid!

Penny Larkin (10)
Moorcroft Wood Primary School, Bilston

JACKY CHAN LESSON

Racing back from work, I saw a sign saying: If you want a lesson from a person called Jacky Chan, you may have to travel to China.

On my journey to China, I spotted a dangerous species sliding across the huge narrow road.

Soon I had learnt my lesson from Jacky Chan. Eventually I had to race all the way home.

I stepped out of my Ferrari F50 and karate chopped the deformed alien because he hurt my Ferrari.

Leighton Tenn (10)
Moorcroft Wood Primary School, Bilston

THE GIANT WAVE

Shining bright, the sun beamed down on the crystal sand. I was relaxing under a palm tree, when suddenly a huge wave crashed onto the beach. I had no time to run. It dragged me into the water.

About half an hour later, I found myself on the sea floor. I sat up confused. I looked round, it was the most wonderful thing I had ever seen. I could breathe. I realised I must be a mermaid!

Sophie Carter (11)
Moorcroft Wood Primary School, Bilston

MY DAY LIVING IN PARIS

When I got off the metro, I saw a load of people on the bus, coming from Manchester to Paris to see the Eiffel Tower.

Whilst I was waiting for the queue to go down, I went to see if there were any shops. I looked around and I saw a subway.

After a while I went to see if I could get in. There I saw a clear shape, so I walked in and there were approximately 147 bronze steps there!

Ryan Gray (10)
Moorcroft Wood Primary School, Bilston

GOING AROUND EGYPT

Slacking inside the vast warm house everyone else was outside in the faded snow. I was dreaming that I was in an arid and hectic place to explore Egypt. I saw the dusty considerable pyramid, tiptoeing inside the gloomy pyramid there were no torches. Uninhibitedly, I crouched quietly. Immediately I saw a diamond, it wouldn't fit in my pocket so I took half then I heard a screaming noise ... it was a mummy! Quick as a flash I woke up!

Adrian Evans (10)
Moorcroft Wood Primary School, Bilston

DISAPPEARING FOREVER

Sinead was a beautiful girl who had brown, shiny hair. She had always wanted to go to Egypt. She went to Egypt and went into the moonless creepy tomb. She was so scared she could not even open her eyes. However, she had a peep and felt brave then opened her eyes wider.
Suddenly she saw a huge pack of zombies and mummies coming towards her. She ran off for her life and kicked the door open and escaped!

Rebecca Porter (10)
Moorcroft Wood Primary School, Bilston

TRIP TO FRANCE

Waking up as normal but it wasn't the same because I was going on an adventure I was going to France, at 1am. I got an aeroplane to France. It took 3 hours to get there.

When I landed I explored France, then I went to the Eiffel Tower. Instead of going up by the lift I climbed a ladder.

One hour later I'd made it up to the dark sky then I flew back home.

Owen Perry (10)
Moorcroft Wood Primary School, Bilston

TRAVELLING UNDERNEATH THE SEA

Shattered, I swam under the sea nervously I saw a gaunt man. Worriedly I asked him what he was doing. Nervously he replied, 'Having a little search around, looking what sort of creatures are underneath here.'

Hastily I got to the middle of the sea and all that time I finally found a stingray and a starfish. Panting, I passed a shark and shot him in the back and watched him drown.

Finally I swam to an island.

John Smallman (10)
Moorcroft Wood Primary School, Bilston

THE BOAT TRIP TO THE NORTH POLE

One day Emilia went on a boat sailing trip to the North Pole. After she went on-board she had a snack on the deck, there was an outstanding view.

After 20 miles Emilia saw an enormous iceberg. Also on top of it there was a polar bear and a seal lion, she was shocked.

After arriving in the North Pole she went for a walk on the snow with her new camera. Shockingly, she caught a glimpse of Santa!

Chloé Selman (10)
Moorcroft Wood Primary School, Bilston

A TALKING SPONGE

Astonished, amazed, shocked, I went diving under the sea in sunny Hawaii. I saw this yellow soft sponge talk.

'Hold still!' he muttered. I was close to fainting, before I did he shot me with a drug.

Amazed, when I woke up, I was a sponge! Io asked the other sponge why I had transformed. He said, 'Whoever sees me has to become a sponge. But you go to the surface, you will become a human again!'

Luke Beighton (10)
Moorcroft Wood Primary School, Bilston

SEE THE GENIE!

I was walking to the airport, I was going to get on the plane I wanted to go to Paris to see the catacombs that I had been waiting to see for 8 years.

Arriving at Paris, I met a genie. So surprised I could not speak! He then sighed, 'You have three wishes, go!'

Then I replied, 'I wish for a horse and that's it.

He disappeared, leaving a horse. However, I couldn't see the catacombs now!

Emily Trueman (10)
Moorcroft Wood Primary School, Bilston

THE MYSTERY PLACE

Swiftly I tiptoed through the soft sound of birds, swaying through the trees like a fox leaping through the fields. I fell into a hole of leaves then a glimmer of light shot out like a tomato shoot. Quickly, I scraped all the leaves out of the way. However I heard shouting, 'Come on put some effort into your dancing.'

I went to investigate. I found out it was a professional dance school. Louie Spence was teaching them.

Lauren Hopcroft (10)
Moorcroft Wood Primary School, Bilston

78

DYNAMO AND MAGIC

When I turn on the TV and put on the channel, I go into a world of my own.

I watch Dynamo and his amazing tricks with fire, bottles, walking through glass and amazing card tricks. He is the best magician throughout the whole world and can do magic when they lean back, not supported. Dynamo found his magician when he was picked on at school. He spread out his body weight so they couldn't pick him up.

Bradley Jones (10)
Moorcroft Wood Primary School, Bilston

THE CLOUD JOURNEY

Waking up with a horrible feeling I opened my silky curtains and looked out of my bedroom window looking up into the deep blue sky and I wondered if I could go on an adventure.

I jumped out of my bedroom window, onto a fluffy white cloud and then the cloud took me to Paris and I saw the big Eiffel Tower. I was stupid to pay to go up there.

It was a dream, I woke up!

Kloe Carter (10)
Moorcroft Wood Primary School, Bilston

UNTITLED

I sat down on the Hawaii beaches. Looking up at the sky. Wonder what would be happening soon. Suddenly a boat came over; no one there. I looked around. I saw a shiny object. I looked closely, only a shell! I walked onto the boat. Then it moved around Hawaii. I tried to drive back but it wouldn't let me. So I sat down, nervous for what would happen. Suddenly it stopped, it ended up on the beach!

Chelsea Yu (11)
New Invention Junior School, Willehall

THE DRAGON OF DINYS EMRYS

As I took my very first step into the cave of Dinys Emyrs, I was so nervous that my palms were sweating. My eyesight was melting like ice cream in the sun. I don't know why but I could sense my lost look coming. But before I could finish that thought a red mystical dragon popped out of nowhere. My heart raced like a football team in a relegation battle. I caught a glimpse of a golden box full of treasure!

Owen Dean Bennison (8)
Oakham Primary School, Oldbury

MY EXPEDITION TO DINYS EMRYS

I took my first few footsteps into the inky dark cave. My knees were wobbling and I was biting my lips. The darkness was as black as night. Even though I didn't want to go into the cave, I did.
Suddenly I heard a noise. What was it? It had red, ruby eyes, silver, gleaming claws and scaly skin. It was a dragon. My eyes glimpsed some golden treasure. Would I defeat the dragon or suffer? What would I do?

Rajan Aulakh (8)
Oakham Primary School, Oldbury

THE DRAGON OF DINAS EMRYS

I'm taking my first footstep of the dark gloomy cave of Dinas Emrys. I took the last look at the bright light. *Why am I here?* I thought. Suddenly a red, ruby dragon appeared. It was the dragon of Dinas Emrys. His bright eyes were as bright as the sun. He breathed fire hotter than lava. I'm badly hurt by his claws as sharp as butcher's knives. I was stabbing the dragon then I saw golden, gleaming, glistening gold!

Jack Fletcher (8)
Oakham Primary School, Oldbury

THE DRAGON'S CAVE

As I entered the deep cave I had a look around. Then my sword dropped on the floor with a spark of fire. I picked my sword and saw a dragon! I ran and ran over skulls and swords and stopped on top of the dragonhead. Then I climbed into the dragon's mouth and pulled my sword into the dragon's jaw and smiled. Then I plunged my sword out of the jaw and the dragon died.

Emily Barnes (8)
Oakham Primary School, Oldbury

UNTITLED

I took my first footsteps into the old cave. I looked behind for the last time. The bushes were swishing, Dinas Emrys was pitch-black. Freezing, lonely black. Who was going to be there? I did not have time to answer. Within a second the eyes were like huge diamonds. I got out my sword as the dragon came closer. I saw a glimpse of the golden treasure. So I went to the dragon and killed it.

Sophia Sandhu (8)
Oakham Primary School, Oldbury

THE DRAGON OF DINAS EMRYS

As I took my first step into the cave my life was doomed. Should I run back or should I carry on? Dinas Emrys was a place of death, I gulped. My lip quivered, my heart pounded. Nothing could stop me. The darkness took away the light. The door shut tight, something was wrong. The fire came rushing towards me! It was hot, red and orange. I caught a glimpse of golden, glorious and gleaming treasure. I couldn't reach it!

Grace Stephanie Calloway (8)
Oakham Primary School, Oldbury

THE DRAGON'S DEN

I took my first step to the cave of Dinas Emrys. I heard screaming. 'Please help!' someone wailed. I heard screeching crumbling and munching. As blood splattered over my face I then slipped on a rock! Then I saw a bunch of eyes. What is it?
It didn't take me long to answer that question. A roaring dragon came …

James Debney (9)
Oakham Primary School, Oldbury

83

THE DRAGON OF DINYS EMRYS

I took tiny footsteps inside the deep, dark, wet cave. I was frightened; my heart broke to pieces and dropped. Before me stood a red, evil dragon breathing fire angrily. Then I went to fight the dangerous dragon and won. My sword was ready to plunge the dragon, real hard. Dinys Emrys is a nasty place with a dragon. The dragon's flames flew towards me as fast as lightning. Water dripped from the cold, dark, creepy cave like rain.

Millie Boyes (8)
Oakham Primary School, Oldbury

THE DRAGON OF DINYS EMRYS

As I stepped into the spooky cave of Dinys Emrys, it felt like the ceiling was collapsing. I turned around and whispered, 'Goodbye light.' Outside the grass swayed like hair in the wind. The trees stood like statues. Should I walk on? *The treasure is mine now dragon!* shouts a voice in my mind. I'm scared like an ant so crept down by a rock. I heard something. I saw the dragon and the gold. Should I run?

Noah Gilbert (8)
Oakham Primary School, Oldbury

DRAGON OF DINYS EMRYS

As I entered the Dinys Emrys' cave I looked behind my shoulder to take the last glimpse of sunlight. I walked deeper into the cave, I was nervous. The cave was as black as a bat. Suddenly I saw a mouse on fire! I got the feeling a dragon was close.

I kept saying to myself, 'Should I have entered?' I walked further into the cave. My heart beat and my knees quivered, I wondered what would happen next.

Liyah Dhinsa (9)
Oakham Primary School, Oldbury

DINYS EMRYS

I entered the Dinys Emrys cave. I had a stick of fire. Suddenly I saw a shadow among the rocks. I was scared; all I could hear was my feet squelching in the water. Then I saw some smoke; it was as grey as a grey crayon. I thought to myself, *shall I carry on or run back like a wuss?* I decided to carry on. I saw the dragon, I pulled my sword out and I saw gold …

Jack Male (8)
Oakham Primary School, Oldbury

THE DRAGON OF DINYS EMRYS

As I entered the cave I gasped at the darkness. I took my first footstep. I shivered like a bag of jelly. I was worried like a scaredy-cat. Then I saw a bulging green eye. What was it? It came out. Then my heart skipped a beat. I heard a roar. I questioned myself, should I be a wimp and run or be brave and fight? I chose bravery and the treasure.
I started my battle, I won!

Morgan Westwood (8)
Oakham Primary School, Oldbury

THE ADVENTURE IN MERLIN'S CAVE

I took my first steps into the frosty cave of Dinas Emrys. My knees shook and I bit my lip. I slowly walked into the pitch-black cave. What could possibly go wrong? I saw a gigantic red figure! Should I go towards it? Should I run? What to do? Look! Was I sure I saw a dragon? I saw some gold, shiny treasure! I swung my sword here and there at the dragon. But it was just too fast …

Keira Hopkins (8)
Oakham Primary School, Oldbury

THE GREAT DRAGON OF DINYS EMRYS

As I entered the dusty cave it was dark, cold and lonely. The cave took away the light and brought on the dark. The trees stood still like motionless statues. What was waiting for me at Dinys Emrys? I didn't have long to answer that question because suddenly there was a pair of crystal eyes. The flame lit up the cave but I got a glimpse of golden sparkly treasure. It sparkled like a star. The dragon was absolutely huge!

Reggie Jones (9)
Oakham Primary School, Oldbury

THE DRAGON OF DINAS EMRYS

I stepped into the dark cave. I took a deep breath and took my last look behind me. The trees stood like crooked statues. I was now alone. Should I run or not, Dinas Emrys? I did not have long to answer the question. Within seconds, the crystal eyes of the fiercest dragon broke the gloom. I ripped out my sword and screamed for the best. As the dragon's fire came even closer to me, I caught glimpses of treasure …

Libby Bailey (8)
Oakham Primary School, Oldbury

UNTITLED

I took my first baby footsteps in the dark, horrible cave. When I was holding a light I heard a noise so I moved my light around and … there was a dragon! I dropped my light on the floor and screamed loudly. I tried to set the place on fire but I couldn't. The dragon stepped forward, closer to me. I thought, *what is he going to do to me?* So I got a tooth out his jaw, never again!

Charlene Windmill (8)
Oakham Primary School, Oldbury

ALONE ON THE STREETS!

'Come on,' exclaimed Rosie. 'We really have to find some food from somewhere or we will starve to death!'
'But why can't we stay here overnight?' whined Alfie.
'Here on the streets?' Rosie answered surprised.
'You mean with people, houses and what I think they call animals or something like that anyway?
Alfie and Rosie had not had much life experience or neither knew what many things or objects were in the world. The world was a big place!

Grace Joesbury (10)
Oakham Primary School, Oldbury

WHAT IS IT?

'Argh!' I just woke up from my terrible dream thinking that I got kidnapped in Portugal, even though I could hear guns shooting and people screaming. But oh no! It was just my brother playing Saints Row. So I went back to bed until I heard another noise creaking and whispering. I opened my bedroom door to see what it was, but it was just my toy robot walking around.
Phew, what a scary frightening day, I have had!'

Misbah Choudhury (11)
Oakham Primary School, Oldbury

PYRAMID GHOST

I'm flying on a plane to Egypt. It's 4 hours long.
I'm finally there, it is hot, I need some water. I'm glad I did. I like it here but the only thing is money. I run to collect some money but then I notice now that no one is in the town but me and the big pyramids. I hear a sound, I'm scared. I feel a slight touch on my shoulder but I know no one's there!

Katie Jones (10)
Oakham Primary School, Oldbury

REMEMBERED BY MANY PEOPLE!

As 22-year-old James Parker steps out of the plane, it's like the world has frozen in front of him. He knows he has to do his best in the next three weeks as he has just entered London for the Olympics. James is a swimmer.

As he is walking down the steps of the plane he falls. *Crash, bang.*

'Ooh!' Then silence.

He wakes up in the hospital. He missed the Olympics, but was famous forever onwards!

Georgia Hill (10)
Oakham Primary School, Oldbury

VOLCANOES AROUND THE WORLD

There are many types of volcanoes around the world but not just on this planet, there are some volcanoes on mats, that's what them lumps are. There are also volcanoes in really cold conditions. Advice: if you get to see a volcano stay quite safe because if it erupts (explodes) you won't be able to escape the lava because the extreme heat will melt you. You know if it's erupting because the ground shakes. Will you live or die?

Jake (10)
Oakham Primary School, Oldbury

I WILL THINK NEXT TIME!

I was asked to go in a competition. I thought it was a running race so I said, 'Yes.' I was told to be there on the 8th November.
Two weeks before, I started training for running.
On the 8th November I went. It looked unusual. It was a wrestling match! I was mad with myself for practising running. Unfortunately, I lost! Next time I apply for a competition I'll check what it is for!

Chloe Beswick (10)
Oakham Primary School, Oldbury

THE ULTIMATE SACRIFICE

I'm perched with a sniper, inspecting the Nazi army. 'All is silent. Over!' I say into the walkie talkie. I finally decide to intercept in Hitler's speech.
'And now, bow down before your new general!' I steadied my aim, and shot the general. A soldier spotted me and they released the K-9 unit. I run from the dogs gnashing at my feet but it was no use. A dog bit my leg and floored me. I killed the general. Why?

George Collier (10)
Oakham Primary School, Oldbury

I WISH ...

My life was going to change forever. It was a Tuesday so I was going to school. I went walking down to school. I thought, *I'm broke! I wished I had some money.*

Suddenly a 50-pound note came towards me. I thought it was lucky but I was wrong.

All day when I said, 'I wish' I got something.

When I got home I had an argument with my mum. I wished for something that I shouldn't have done!

Lauren Berry (10)
Oakham Primary School, Oldbury

JAKE

Jake was a farmer who lived in Australia. He lived in a town where everyone was the best of friends. The river where he got his water from has stopped flowing. The crops started dying and people did too without any food.

One day he went up the river to get the water. The water dried up so he decided to go up a mountain to look for water. He pushed snow down to melt and get water there.

Nathan Gallagher (10)
Oakham Primary School, Oldbury

THE MAN WHO GOT LOST

Matt, an explorer, loved going into the rainforest, but got lost once. He was on a quad bike going to the rainforest and he went extremely fast.

When he went into the heart of the rainforest he got off his quad bike and got his machete out and went further in.

After a few hours he came back and saw his quad bike completely smashed by animals. He killed most of them but then he got killed.

Bradley Davies (11)
Oakham Primary School, Oldbury

UNTITLED

Deep down in Australia Chris, who adored animals, went to search for koala bears and somehow got lost in the rainforest.

As the day went by the trees laughed as Chris begun to panic. Watching the sky transform itself from day to night he decided that he wasn't gonna give up until he got out.

Finally, the next day, Chris was really tired. Suddenly he saw bright lights and thought, *could this be it?* No, it couldn't …

Paige Murphy (10)
Oakham Primary School, Oldbury

AN UNEXPECTED DIP

It started out like any other day for Conner at Australia Zoo. First, the morning show, every day Conner performed the croc show. But today it went wrong! Conner held out the tender meat for the beast of a croc. It dived deep down. The audience waited in anticipation. The croc propelled from the bottom. Splash! The croc took Conner down. Conner battled with the beast, spinning until he could wrestle it to the bottom and capture it. A spectacular show!

Oliver Haydon (10)
Oakham Primary School, Oldbury

THE COMA

I walk down the road where she got hit. It was always busy, not the best place to cross. I stopped and looked at the crossing. I closed my eyes and there we were.
We were walking down the road in Birmingham. I turned my head. 'Don't!' she said but I ran. She followed me but so did a car. I managed to escape but she didn't. I could imagine her in her hospital bed covered by a white quilt.

Ellisia Williams (10)
Oakham Primary School, Oldbury

THE GIRL'S NIGHTMARE

Just then I opened the door and … a German clown! Let's go to the start. I was invited to my best friend's birthday party. I was so excited; it was like I was going to explode. I was on my way and then I saw where the party was, a big posh Spanish hotel!
Just then I opened the door and a German clown! I'm scared, I tried to run out but the door wouldn't open. It was locked!
'Argh!'

Simrit Kaur (10)
Oakham Primary School, Oldbury

OUR GOOD SERGEANT

We're here now in Paris. Waiting for Soap's orders to give him coverfire for when he moves into the hotel. But suddenly everything changes the buildings explode and we're falling. We hit the ground hard but we're alright and looking for Soap.
We've found him but he's in a bad shape.
We're fighting our way through the city. We're fighting a losing battle. We get back to our base but it's too late. RIP Sergeant Soap, your country is proud.

Conner Langford (11)
Oakham Primary School, Oldbury

THE PLANE WE MISSED!

Paris, the city of love.
'We're going on a honeymoon,' shouted Mum in my room at six this morning.
The luggage is already packed so huddle into the taxi.
'We're late,' Mum shouted.
We were at the airport. Our clocks were never put forward at home. We rushed and rushed but it didn't turn out lovey dovey for Mum and Dad because we never made the plane to Paris … the city of love.

Abbie Gilbert (11)
Oakham Primary School, Oldbury

THE SHARK ATTACK

'Sally, go lie your flowers by the grave,' said Mrs Cooper. Tears began to flow as the body got lowered into the ground.
It all started when the beach began to fill up with tourists. The children loved the sea, that meant I needed to watch, sharks had caused attacks. A little girl named Mandy was in the water! The shark came closer! I ran! The girl survived!
'Please, please somebody help me!'
But sadly I was too late.

Sophie Morton (10)
Oakham Primary School, Oldbury

THE WALLABY RESCUE

'G'day Keith,' said Karl.
'G'day Karl,' said Keith.
'Who's that over there?' whispered Karl.
'It's Craig the crocodile,' said Keith.
Craig rushed towards Wayne, the wallaby, ready for his first meal in four hours. Keith and Karl risked their lives and rushed towards Craig and Wayne who were very small. Keith saved Wayne, while Karl kicked Craig in his face. Luckily, Karl miraculously survived. Karl then made friends with Wayne and they went home to Keith's grassy bamboo stalk.

Callum Howard (10)
Oakham Primary School, Oldbury

A BOAT THAT GOT LOST

Paul, who had a boat, lived in the lovely countryside with man cute animals, also some nice lovely houses. One day he took his boat out into the sea on a windy day.
Suddenly a big storm came along and blew him straight into the centre of the sea. Terrified he was stuck in the centre of the sea where no one could find him. Nobody could help him. He had to swim back and leave his boat alone.

Aaron Rix (11)
Oakham Primary School, Oldbury

UNTITLED

This girl who loves exploring wants to go into the forest. Her parents are very strict though. Unexpectedly, the girl's parents had to go out she saw her chance.

When her parents were out of sight she made her way to the forest. She reached the forest and took her first steps slowly. She was deep in the forest and heard a snake. She turned and there it was. It quickly wiped itself around her. She screamed, struggling for breath.

Amelia Marks (10)
Oakham Primary School, Oldbury

POLLY AND HER KANGAROO

Polly, who is an animal loving girl, had the best friend anyone could ever have, Joey a kangaroo. Polly began to cry; she could not find Joey anywhere. She searched for days but no hope. So went looking in the outback.

Polly wasn't seen for weeks. People thought she had died but unknown to them Joey was behind the shed. He heard everything so he went searching for Polly. Joey found Polly alive and carried her all the way home.

Megan Hawley (11)
Oakham Primary School, Oldbury

A SAFE PLACE

Holly and Ben who are very excited, are going on a school trip. They are going to the Australian Outback. As they were walking around the park, Ben felt ill. He felt as hot as fire and had to sit down on a rock.
Holly shouted, 'Ben, there's a snake under that rock.' The teacher said, 'Make lots of noise to frighten the snake away.' Then said, 'It's too dangerous here, let's go back to school where it is safer.'

Charlie Louise Gethen (11)
Oakham Primary School, Oldbury

ADVENTURING AUSTRALIA

'Sssh, Dumbo, we are in a vast rainforest definitely infested by aborigines, dangerous animals and cannibals,' whispered Owen, the dumbest. Both of them, who were both adventurers, had loads of bad things happen to them. First it was being wrapped by an anaconda, then being bitten by a redback spider. After, it was being kicked by a kangaroo, being hit round the head with a boomerang and being stabbed by an arrow. Unfortunately Owen got killed by everything that happened.

Korben Johnson (10)
Oakham Primary School, Oldbury

LIVE IN AUSTRALIA

Tom, a geologist in Australia, was captured by aborigines. He was terrified. Tom, all tied up lonely, struggled, trapped. He then heard footsteps getting louder and louder. He then saw the chief of the colonies, Hoomulur. He sentenced Tom to death by fire but Tom escaped the fiery inferno and back to England to report his findings.

A week later Tom returned with back-up. He captured all the aboriginals. They were under his power.

Lucas Robinson (10)
Oakham Primary School, Oldbury

THE CHAOTIC REVENGE

Nick, who is an animal skinner, trudged through the darkness of the forest. Just then a misty creature came out! Nick pulled out his dagger. Then it charged at Nick! He was paralysed with little strength. His vision was blurry but he was in his hometown, Sydney, 60,000 years ago, surrounded by fierce creatures. He let out a last yelp then silence.

He was known from then on as the unsuccessful poacher!

Oliver Chilton (10)
Oakham Primary School, Oldbury

THE DRAGON OF DINYS EMRYS

I took my first step, might be my last, into the dark gloomy cave. I took a glimpse into the cave. The trees looked like old, crouched women. It kept getting darker every step. I felt like a man alone in a war zone. Dinys Emrys seemed scary.

Suddenly I saw orange on the wall. It was a dragon. I ran and hoped he didn't see me. I cut off his toe and ran cautiously to get the golden treasure.

Joshua Bates (8)
Oakham Primary School, Oldbury

THE ITALIAN GHOST

Legend says that Italy has a ghost waiting for the right person. A girl called Sarah went to Italy with her grandparents. The day she got there she went to the park.

She got to the park and nobody was there. She went on the swings. Then, all of a sudden, her swing stopped and the other moved. Her nan shouted her and she replied OK. She tried to move but it was like someone was holding her down forever!

Ellie Cotton (10)
Oakham Primary School, Oldbury

THE WONDERFUL PLACES TO GO!

Hi there, I'm James and I've always wanted to go around the world! It seems so fun!

So there I was getting into the silver speedy car. I drove the vehicle at 100mph, I needed to get to the airport.

I got on the first humongous aeroplane to Rome! 'Wow! Romans!'

Next stop, Greece. I'm literally speechless, astonished!

India, the food was way too lovely!

Aww, back home now too bad! But I have to say what an amazing journey!

Karina Sanghera (10)
St Martin's CE Primary School, Tipton

NIGHTMARE IN LONDON

Round and round London until my feet felt numb. There it was! The thing I hadn't seen in a long time, Big Ben! *Ding-dong!* I ran as fast as I could. It was only once I had looked back that it was only the bell. Next time I come to London, I will not go so close to the 'scary' Big Ben!

Chloe Lane (10)
St Martin's CE Primary School, Tipton

THE LONG CLIMB

I was climbing a huge monster, kicking a rock. I looked down, it was like a never-ending drop. Bounce went the rock off a giant bit of rock. Higher and higher I climbed, painfully my legs aching and aching. I looked around and saw a beautiful view but I knew I had to go even further. My clothes were getting heavier and my legs dragged behind. I was getting nearer to the top of Mount Everest. I'd reached it.

Caitlin Perkins (11)
St Martin's CE Primary School, Tipton

VIC THE VIPER VS TWISTER TORNADO

The lights go down and the excited crowd are ready to see some wrestling. Twister Tornado body slams Vic the Viper to the ground. Vic the Viper comes back with his signature move, the Viper Strike. Now Twister Tornado is mad and unleashes his signature move, The Gruesome Gas Bomb. Is Vic the Viper out for the count? One, two, three, four, five – *ding, ding, ding!* Round over, Twister Tornado wins and the crowd goes wild.

Cavan Connor Martin-Jones (10)
St Martin's CE Primary School, Tipton

THE EIFFEL TOWER

I was at the Eiffel Tower in France and I went up in the colossal lift. I was looking forward to seeing the amazing sight. Woohoo! I couldn't wait and I was so excited. Just then … the lift stopped! My adrenaline was pumping fast but fortunately I realised I was at the top. That was a relief. Despite me being scared that the lift stopped! I saw the amazing view and it was worth the really hard-earned cash.

Thomas Hodson (11)
St Martin's CE Primary School, Tipton

I'M A GIRL, GET ME OUT OF SCHOOL!

I'm a girl called Paige and I absolutely hate school (which is not true really!) Miss Scar had a gigantic scar on her neck from a mosquito bite. We eat cockroaches, spiders and beetles. My friend Jaws has bigger teeth than a shark. Miss Scar has wrinkles on her face which means I don't even want to look at her smelly, ugly feet. *Please get me out!*

Paige Henry (10)
St Martin's CE Primary School, Tipton

LOST LIST

One night Santa was delivering presents for the children. Then suddenly the wind blew his list up a chimney. He went in to get it, when he was looking he woke a little girl called Lilly. So Lilly and Santa looked and saw it at the top of the tree, Santa got his list and Lilly got her present, it was a little doll named Petal that she played with all day.
Today Lilly is really, really happy.

Kyra Leigh Buckley (9)
St Martin's CE Primary School, Tipton

THE MAGIC CARPET

Once there was a girl called Sophie and she had a magic carpet. Next door, there was a girl called Gemma. She was jealous of Sophie and that magic carpet too.
One day, Gemma went into Sophie's room and jumped on the magic carpet. Before she could say anything, the magic carpet whooshed up into the sky. Then dropped back down to Sophie's bedroom and Gemma jumped off the magic carpet and ran. She won't do that again!

Francesca Ellis (9)
St Martin's CE Primary School, Tipton

EVIL SANTA

On a cold Christmas Eve in the North Pole lived a man dressed in black, he was called Fanta, he was the evil half brother of Santa. He ran Santa out of business with an evil machine where you have no presents and a Santa election. Kids loved Fanta until, in 2012, he got mean and killed all the reindeer. Nobody got any presents.

On a crispy Christmas night Fanta was on his daily jog when he slipped and sank!

William Gill (10)
St Martin's CE Primary School, Tipton

THE HAUNTED HOUSE

I was forced to go in this huge house. I was completely scared, all the windows had spiderwebs. I ran up the creaky stairs and ran into a room – lock myself in. I switched the lights on but they wouldn't come on, I was sweating. I jumped out the window, hurting my leg; I walked alone to the hospital.

The next day I went home and went to bed. I dreamt of a fierce enormous green, orange dragon.

Seynab Abdullahi (9)
The Oval Primary School, Birmingham

THE MIGHTY BLIZZARD

When I woke up I couldn't open my eyes. I was stuck in a mighty blizzard with my crew. We were trying to get to the South Pole but the lightning struck and killed my two best companions. I saw something in the distance, I couldn't make the picture out as it was blurred from the blizzard, but it was coming closer and every time it came closer it got clearer …

Riyadh Kibria (9)
The Oval Primary School, Birmingham

UNTITLED

I was climbing the pyramids of Egypt when a sandstorm took place. I felt as hot as a jalapeno. I needed water, my throat was as dry as sandpaper. I saw a palm tree with a pond underneath and camels right next to it. I ran and ran. I ran up to the water, but it just disappeared. I was in the middle of the desert surrounded by nothing but sand. 'I am so thirsty. What happens to me now?'

Halima Amin (9)
The Oval Primary School, Birmingham

THE NORTHERN LIGHTS

There were green, purple, orange, red, pink fantastic swirls in the sky; all different colours. I asked my mom what they were, she said, 'They're called the Northern Lights.' I've never seen anything like it before, it was beautiful. My favourite colour was orange, bursting with colour. I absolutely loved them, they were the most beautiful thing I'd ever seen. They were almost like fireworks but better. They were on the news and reporters said they were most amazing.

Katie Louise Green (9)
The Oval Primary School, Birmingham

THE MYSTERY TREASURE

Me and my crew were sailing on the Indian ocean, we were sailing on our old, dusty sambuk. I was looking out for treasure, so we went to an isolated island. Me and my crew stepped on the beach, one of my mates stood on a sparkling shell. A secret door opened beneath us, we all went in as we weren't scared. There was sand everywhere. I dug up the middle and I saw it there glowing …

Isa Hussain (10)
The Oval Primary School, Birmingham

THE DANGEROUS STORY

I went to a cave with a dragon inside and went in. I put the light on and touched the dragon's nose – he loved and liked me! He let me get on his back and we took to the sky for a training flight. We flew for hours – quick as a blink. Suddenly there was another dragon coming to attack the friendly dragon. He fought back and killed him with one mighty bite.

Hayden Parkinson (9)
The Oval Primary School, Birmingham

THE WRONG TURN

We were heading for the North Pole but it went wrong. The plane crashed and we were in the wrong destination ... When I woke up I grabbed hold of the plane wing and pulled myself up – I was deserted. I saw a pyramid and ran there. I fell down a hole. There was the golden skull, with blue glowing eyes and red pupils. There were the other survivors holding the golden skull ...

Layton O'Brien (9)
The Oval Primary School, Birmingham

THE SHELL

I was here at the hotel, all the colours and the lights
– I was in the Big Apple. I saw the Statue of Liberty.
I was right by the statue. I stepped in the sea and I
found a shell, I took it home. I saw a crown, I put it
on.
The next day I went swimming and I saw Atlantis and
I became a mermaid and I was the Queen of the sea.

Abigail Fearby (9)
The Oval Primary School, Birmingham

THE BIG APPLE

Finally I was here! The Big Apple. I was sweating from
head to toe. I tried to cool myself down by going into
my sparkling pool with a drink as cold as a snowman
with a fancy little blue umbrella. I was swimming then
suddenly a flash beamed under the water, I looked
and I saw a fish tail. From that moment I knew I was
a mermaid. Every time I touched the water I was a
mermaid again.

Jessica Paige Hitchins (9)
The Oval Primary School, Birmingham

A MISSION

It was freezing cold and my companions were dying one by one. There were only two left. My lungs were paralysed because the temperature was -35°C. Everything was blurred out by a blizzard. My companions' bodies were covered deep in snow. I could hear a faint noise in the distance. My head was dizzy and my feet were aching. Something was coming towards me. What could it be? ...

Sohail Sattar (9)
The Oval Primary School, Birmingham

CANDYFLOSS LAND

Fluffy was a gigantic monster. He lived in a world made out of candy. The trees were made out of candyfloss with multicoloured fruit and sweets growing. When he was walking from the trees he saw an enormous gingerbread house with brightly coloured windows and a chocolate roof. Suddenly an ugly, terrifying witch captured Fluffy in a dark black net. Fluffy's friend, Munch, came with his sharp, shiny teeth and rescued him. They scampered quickly away from the witch.

Morgan Broadley (8)
Wallbrook Primary School, Coseley

MARSHMALLOW LAND

As I stood in my bedroom I could see my wardrobe. I opened the door and suddenly I landed on a beach. I saw the sun shining on the glittery sand. We saw a shell, we shook it. We landed in Marshmallow Land, it was fun. We couldn't get back. We shook it again it didn't work, there was something stuck inside. We got a marshmallow and ripped it open. Inside was a magic diamond that took us home.

Ellie Broadbent (8)
Wallbrook Primary School, Coseley

THE MAGICAL WOODS

Once there was a lovely brown-coated pup named Sparky. He had a small friend called Kitty. 'What have you been doing?' asked Sparky. No one answered so he said it again. Then he looked behind him … A wizard was running away with Kitty! Sparky followed the wizard to his house. He tried to rescue Kitty but the wizard was too fast. Finally Sparky grabbed the wand and broke it. 'Noooo!' cried the wizard as he melted into slime.

Liberty Large (8)
Wallbrook Primary School, Coseley

CHOCOLATE MAN

Once there was a chocolate man, he had a chocolate house and lived in Chocolate Land. He went to play with his enormous football with peanuts inside. Then he went on a chocolate trampoline, he was jumping in the sky. Suddenly he fell into the chocolate duck pond. His chocolate brother came to rescue him. He pulled and pulled but he slipped and fell in too! They sat there laughing and decided to go for a swim instead.

Kyril Chavula (8)
Wallbrook Primary School, Coseley

CHLOE AND TED

Chloe and Ted were walking through Chocolate Land. They saw a chocolate river. Ted wanted to taste the chocolate. Chloe said it was dangerous and tried to stop Ted but Ted ran and started to eat the chocolate, he slipped and fell in. Ted shouted for help. Chloe came and started to cry. She grabbed a lollipop tree and helped Ted out of the river. Ted gave Chloe a hug and said, 'Thank you for saving me.'

Angel Hill (8)
Wallbrook Primary School, Coseley

THE ADVENTURES OF LITTLE MAN

Little Man had a teddy called Ted. He had dropped him in the river. Ted came to life and he couldn't swim. 'I can't swim,' he shouted.
'I will get some help.'
As she ran into Lee, the monster, he was a nice monster. He grabbed Ted out of the river.

Tyrel Paterson (8)
Wallbrook Primary School, Coseley

THE CANDY LAND ADVENTURE

Bugsy Bouncer stood in Candyfloss Land eating candyfloss carrots. There was nobody to be seen so he kept eating carrots until he got stuck in a mountain of candyfloss. Suddenly, from out of the blue, a flying dog landed on Candyfloss Mountain. Bugsy shouted, 'Help!' the flying dog started to eat the candyfloss. Bugsy was shocked because the dog started to talk. He told Bugsy all about the strawberry lace trees covered in chocolate and cream. 'Yummy!' said Bugsy.

Summer Evans (8)
Wallbrook Primary School, Coseley

FLUFFYLAND

One day a scientist discovered a land called Fluffyland. There was a creature called Fluffymunch who ate red-hot crisps. Every time he walked it sounded like crisps crunching. Nobody liked him because he smelt like rubbish.

One day a big monster was eating the land, nobody did anything. So Fluffymunch got up and tied up the monster and saved the town.

From that day everyone loved him and they called him Supermunch, the hero!

Jamal Handley (9)
Wallbrook Primary School, Coseley

CHOCOLATE WORLD

Once upon a time there was a boy and girl. Their names were Ellie and Leighton and they were very best friends. They saw a mirror and they were in a world called Chocolate World. They saw a river, they went over to it, they tried it and they liked it.

They had some more. They took it home, they ran out of the delicious chocolate and marshmallow land. They got some more.

Leighton Rogers (8)
Wallbrook Primary School, Coseley

DOC AND MARDY'S ADVENTURE

Doc and Mardy were walking along the dark green grass. Doc was on his phone and Mardy saw a teddy in the chocolate river. Doc and Mardy and Ted were walking in the chocolate field. A lady was walking past and grabbed Teddy. Doc and Mardy didn't realise Teddy was gone. They ran to their car to go looking for Teddy. They found him having a picnic in the chocolate field.

Cameron Westbury (8)
Wallbrook Primary School, Coseley

THE MAGICAL FOREST

Before the world began there was a magical forest. One day me and Sweetiepie wandered around the incredible forest. In a flash chocolate trees appeared out of nowhere, rivers, lakes, waterfalls, all made out of chocolate. Then … Sweetiepie flew off, I couldn't find her. After a while I heard a noise, I walked further. I saw a golden eagle. He said he would help me. We searched everywhere for Sweetiepie. Suddenly, I saw a yellow feather. It was her!

Paris Gambone (8)
Wallbrook Primary School, Coseley

FROSTY'S DANGEROUS TRIP

Once there was a snowman called Frosty. He lived in the most snowy world. He wore the biggest top hat and when he sang he flew and when he talked he walked. Everything he ate was cold. Suddenly he fell down the biggest ice hole. He quickly swam to an ice tunnel and dug himself out. A girl saw him trying to get out. She helped him out and they celebrated.

Katie Sherwood (8)
Wallbrook Primary School, Coseley

CHOCOLATE LAND

Fred is a famous chocolate maker. He lives in Chocolate Land. He makes chocolate. He has a fluffy puppy, his name is Leyla and he can talk. He has a cat called Reagan and another cat called Smoky. Fred wears black leather shoes. He wears a black coat.

'Oh no!' said the cat and the dog. 'Fred has fallen into the chocolate river!'

Finally Fred was rescued by the fluffy dog, Leyla and the cats, Reagan and Smoky.

Maddie Kinsey (8)
Wallbrook Primary School, Coseley

A SNOWY ADVENTURE

One day, Fum, the giant, was walking out of his gigantic palace. It was snowing so he went to the underground world. He magicked a limousine. He wanted to check for baddies. He saw one! It was Octeeria the spider. She had bombs so he caught her and threw her five million miles away! He got in the limousine but it snowed more fiercely and he couldn't see so he crashed. His wife, Fem, saved him. They had a party.

Callum Cleaver (8)
Wallbrook Primary School, Coseley

THE CHOCOLATE FIELD

Years ago there was a teddy. He joined the army. The king had lost his crown and diamonds. Teddy wanted to help find them. Teddy went to Chocolate Fields. Suddenly, the chocolate broke under Teddy. He dug with his paws to see what he could find. In the chocolate field he found the king's diamonds and crown. He ran as fast as he could to give the king his things back. The king was happy.

Tyler Pritchard (7)
Wallbrook Primary School, Coseley

THE MONSTER AWARD

Stuart was walking, suddenly, he saw Ted stuck in the bubbling water. Stuart saw a fizzy man, he looked nice. Stuart asked Fizzy Man for help but he said no. fizzy Man ran away because he was scared of the water. Stuart called for help. A friendly monster came and pulled Ted out of the water. Stuart gave the monster a golden gobstopper award for saving Ted.

Lee Garbett (8)
Wallbrook Primary School, Coseley

LITTLE NINJA

There was a little ninja and he hunted for food with a spear. He found a candy world and chocolate horse. There was a teddy screaming for help. He got a bow and arrow and shot the rope around the bear. Little Ninja pulled the bear up so he was out of the chocolate river. The president awarded Little Ninja with a new knife so he could travel across the candy jungle.

George Whiston
Wallbrook Primary School, Coseley

VILLANVILLE

Sam caught the last problem for today at least. 'My work here is done.' It had just begun! A disastrous nightmare had arrived to destroy Villanville. 'Oh no, he's got a bomb to destroy us.'
Suddenly, two people jumped down from the sky. It was … Lee the Lion and Gordn the Ginat. 'Give me my gold back!' in his loudest voice.
'Never!' So he bit his head off and Gordon threw him to China.
'You're our heroes, thank you.'

Jack Preece (8)
Wallbrook Primary School, Coseley

GAME CORRUPTION

On a wet Saturday morning in Steve's bedroom he was playing his Xbox on his favourite game. But he got stuck on a level. He suddenly got angry with his Xbox and hit it. Then he got sucked into his game. he crashed into a tree. 'Where am I?' Steve said. Then an armoured convoy drove past, but then a gun fired, one almost hit him. *Am I in Far Cry 3? How do I get out of here?* wondered Steve.

Finnlee Burrows (9)
Wallbrook Primary School, Coseley

THE DOLPHIN RESCUE

One day two men went fishing and caught a baby dolphin and tried to kill it. They thought that they wanted it fresh so they got a tank and filled it up with water and put the dolphin in. They took the dolphin to their den. Suddenly something came out of the water, they found out that her baby was missing and sensed where it was and rescued it.

Natasha Hudson (9)
Wallbrook Primary School, Coseley

THE HAUNTED MANSION

As the white unicorn stepped into the graveyard it heard a noise. *Clunk.* It ran until it got to a mansion. It stepped inside, the door went crack and bang. The unicorn looked around, it saw something go right in front of its face. It looked around. There was something standing there. The unicorn started chasing the long, dark shadow. The unicorn ran out of the door and ran to the stable and went to the stable. *Bang!*

Adam Cheadle (9)
Wallbrook Primary School, Coseley

LILY-MAY AND THE BIG BLUE MONSTER

As the loudest noise of a dog barking came around the corner the dog came to a cliff. Then the cliff started to fall … the dog fell but then it started to rain and it was dark so the dog called Lily-May, could not see anything. Then a monster ran on the cliff while it was still … cracking. The blue monster fell then he fell on top of him. 'I'm sorry,' said the monster.
'I'm Ok,' said Lily-May.

Kayleigh Round (8)
Wallbrook Primary School, Coseley

THE GINGERBREAD MAN

Once upon a time there lived a gingerbread man in a gingerbread house. He was rocking in his chair when all of a sudden he flung forward and landed straight in the sink. He phoned the ambulance because his arm went down the sink.
They came in an ice cream van. It was very unusual. They baked him another one with chocolate sprinkles and put him back together. Then he married Miss Gingerbread lady and had golden bear children.

Bradley Fisher (9)
Wallbrook Primary School, Coseley

UNTITLED

One thundery night there were two children called Paul and Eloise. Paul said, 'Eloise, let's go in that house.'

'No, we better not. It looks spooky.'

The children went in the round house. They looked around, there was a wall, there was a cracked photo sliding up and down. Then they went in another room, there was a rocking chair. Eloise said, 'Let's get out of here quick!'

It was too late, the door shut with a furious *bang!* …

Harry Brookes (9)
Wallbrook Primary School, Coseley

THE HAPPY DOG

Tiara, the dog, was trotting through the gloomy wood. It ended. Tiara saw a glistening palace but on the bench, quite a distance away, she saw a black figure. The figure chased Tiara into the crystal palace. The figure was glaring at Tiara. Then it vanished!

As Tiara ran further into the palace she saw a body … *Oh*, thought Tiara, *it's only my owner.* Tiara and her owner Sophie had a look around. It took hours. Then they ran home.

Mia-Rae Trubshaw (8)
Wallbrook Primary School, Coseley

THE DREAM

As I wake up a dog is licking me, I get up and I'm in a strange land with purple apples and orange strawberries. I see a dog, it says hello. I am amazed we play games and have fun but then it is time for me to go. I pick some fruit then the branches begin to twist and make a door. Then a man pops out of a hole and gives me a prize. I wake up properly!

Trinity Haworth (9)
Wallbrook Primary School, Coseley

TRAPPED DOG

Once there was a little girl and she had a little cute puppy.
One day the girl let the pup out and there was a broken gate! The pup escaped! 'Daisy, I've got your dinner, it's your favourite.' She walked out the door and gone! No dog! Poor Liberty, her friendship had ended. 'Our friendship hasn't ended because I will put pictures of her all over the streets. I can't wait to find her, we will be together forever.'

Megan Owen (8)
Wallbrook Primary School, Coseley

THE EVIL HEADMASTER

One sunny day a young boy walked through a portal in his back garden, there was a school in the middle of the field, it was a vast size. The boy walked into the school and *bang*, the door slammed shut. He tried to open the door.

'Not so fast!' came a voice.

'Let me out!'

'No!' the headmaster locked him in the cupboard.

He kicked the door. 'Sir, it's raining money.' The headmaster died.

Liam Tibbs (8)
Wallbrook Primary School, Coseley

THE BLUE MERMAID OF THE BLUE SEA

Once there lived a beautiful mermaid that lived in the sea. She had friends in the deep. She helped all her friends, but once the king of sharks was having a fight with the queen of mermaids. The mermaid helped the queen fight the king of the sharks. She got her mermaid friends to help her fight. The day was here.

Hours later she'd done it! She had made the king of sharks go back home. The mermaids had a party.

Hayley Price (8)
Wallbrook Primary School, Coseley

THE UNICORN

The attractive white unicorn galloped up to her owner because there was a big dog like a poodle. The poodle said to the unicorn, 'I want your horn because it is a very lovely colour.' The black spider caught the dog and then the dog sneezed so after that the unicorn went quicker than she did before. The spider was on his web, he was trying to make a black cobweb.

Tanya Collins (9)
Wallbrook Primary School, Coseley

A HOPEFUL RESCUE

As the cheetahs were running fast as light through the valley, they were passing by golden garnets shining in the horizon. There were bronze-coloured birds with twinkling silver beaks but something terrible happened. Jack, one of the cheetahs, fell off a cliff and had been injured by rocks at the bottom. Liam, the other cheetah, was surprised. He ran cautiously to the rocky beach but Jack was nowhere in sight. Suddenly, a call that he recognised. Jack was found.

Nicky Miller (9)
Wallbrook Primary School, Coseley

UNTITLED

Joe and Jess were walking in Central Park. Suddenly a man grabbed Jess then she was gone ... The man got a pocket knife and stabbed her in the arm. Then Joe was pulled in a spooky castle. The picture on one of the walls looked at him. It spoke, it was so freaky. The man took Joe to this room and it had spooky pictures on the cracked wall. Suddenly the wall fell on him loudly ...

Lily Jasper (8)
Wallbrook Primary School, Coseley

UNTITLED

The speeding sound of an attractive glittering unicorn trying to get out of the shackles, damaging the silky wings as the unicorn got weaker. The unicorn said, 'Help, you will pay for what you did!'
The warlock took no notice of the unicorn. Suddenly the ground began to shake. *Rarrr!* Out came a golden animal. The mysterious animal attacked. 'Army attack!' said the warlock. Would the army defeat the animal?

Ashton Martin (9)
Wallbrook Primary School, Coseley

127

THE LOST PUPPY

Once there was a puppy called Mia Rae, her owner was called Megan. They went outside and Megan threw a ball. Mia Rae went to get it. Mia Rae went through the little door and it was full of funny looking things. She ran and drank out of the chocolate river and Megan saw the door and went through it. The dog was gone! It got sucked into a hole. 'Oh no, she has gone somewhere ...'

Eloise Wood (8)
Wallbrook Primary School, Coseley

LAND OF MYTHICAL CREATURES

One sunny morning a boy and a dog fell down a cliff. 'Argh!'
They met a unicorn and a gingerbread man. 'Woof!'
The dog ate the gingerbread man.
'Spit it Sparky,' said Liam. 'We need your help. The goblin wants to kill all mythical creatures.'
'I will.'
That day they set off for the castle. 'We are here.'
The dog pulled him down when the gingerbread man stabbed him.

Vincent Medley (8)
Wallbrook Primary School, Coseley

TIGER AND THE UNDERGROUND MONSTER

One sunny day Tiger, the teddy, woke up and went into the garden and found a hole in the ground. He filled it with soil and up came the soil. Something was going wrong, so Tiger looked in the hole, there was nothing there. Then suddenly there was a head in the ground. Tiger thought it was a monster but it wasn't. It was a rabbit! So Tiger pulled her out and they started to play together with love.

Alliyah Abbasi (7)
Wallbrook Primary School, Coseley

UNTITLED

One day a girl called Ruby woke up in a chocolate world. When she woke, she screamed because she was shocked. She got up and started to look around at all the chocolate. She saw a talking zebra and that was very creepy. Soon it ran after her and she was soon hiding behind a tree out of breath. Then she found a path back all the way back to her house.

Holly Turner (8)
Wallbrook Primary School, Coseley

UNTITLED

One miserable, dark day lived a teddy called Maisy. She lived on the moon, it was cold and spotty. But Maisy wasn't scared at all. It six o'clock at night and Maisy got in her rocket. She pressed the fastest button. 'Blast-off!' she added. She came down to Earth.

'Hello,' said a man. She was scared to reply. Maisy found the rainbow. She followed the rainbow. It went higher of the ground. She found it.

Angel Jones (7)
Wallbrook Primary School, Coseley

UNTITLED

One attractive morning I woke up in a jungle and was walking slowly down. When I saw a little girl! I walked to her and asked her what her name was. Her name was Molly, she was magic. She could turn invisible and see through people! Often Molly would just sit in the jungle all lonely and sad. But she took me on an adventure and we became friends. She took me to Florida, we lived there for five days.

Alex Park (7)
Wallbrook Primary School, Coseley

DEEP IN THE JUNGLE

One morning some people crashed in the jungle. I turned invisible because I was wondering who they were. They got out of the plane and they said they would split up.

After a little while my powers were running out so I had to pretend I was someone on the plane. Soon I met everybody, I told them I could turn invisible. They were shocked and they told me the plane crashed. I fixed it and they went home.

Sian Lovett (8)
Wallbrook Primary School, Coseley

UNTITLED

Once there was a dancing boy and he danced everywhere because he loved dancing. Another thing, I was his friend. One day John went through the wood and he did a handstand. He saw a gigantic tree and he thought he could dance up the tree. He actually fell down it! I called the ambulance and he had to go to hospital. After a couple of days he was back on his feet dancing!

Olivia Skyrme (7)
Wallbrook Primary School, Coseley

UNTITLED

Once there was a magical girl called Bella. She didn't have to do anything. She could stretch where she wanted to go. One day she woke up and ate her breakfast. All she had was one tiny sausage and one cornflake.

After a while she heard people shouting. She stretched far across and she saw a building on fire. She got the people and brought them down. They said, 'Thank you.' She stretched back and was very proud of herself.

Lauren Park (7)
Wallbrook Primary School, Coseley

UNTITLED

One day a ball hit a kid's leg and he got a free kick and scored a penalty. Everybody cheered for him. There was a battle going on around the ground and the Avengers were fighting against the bad guys who were attacking the kid and the players. The kid kicked the ball at the bad guys and sent them back into space where they came from.

Josh Smith (7)
Wallbrook Primary School, Coseley

WHAT A DAY

As I ploughed the snow I bumped into an old man, he said, 'Beware, green penguins are getting revenge.' There was a bang. A green penguin just bombed my snow plough. There were penguins all around me, then the old man came and shot one of the penguins but it got back up. There was one way to solve this, catch them and put them in the ocean that's always frozen. Two hours later they were all trapped forever.

George Plant (10)
Woodthorpe Primary School, Birmingham

TREASURE TIME

I walked down the stairs, through bending passages. I thought I would never make it to the bottom, but still I carried on going. It was cold and dark, it was so cold that I thought I might have frostbite then I came to what I wanted to see – Tutankhamun's tomb. There were hieroglyphics all around me. Gold and silver twinkled around the room, goblets, bracelets and even a mummified cat. Pyramids are very beautiful places to see.

Georgina Megan Hood (9)
Woodthorpe Primary School, Birmingham

THE RISE OF ATLANTIS!

My llama and me travelled somewhere. The first thing I did was find a beach. I got to the Great Barrier Reef. I jumped in the sea and found a secret path. The path led me to Atlantis and suddenly, it started to shake. Then it started to shine and blinded me. Before my eyes Atlantis started to float to the surface. Atlantis has never been revealed, so I swam to the surface and pushed it to the bottom.

Simrandeep Singh Chana (9)
Woodthorpe Primary School, Birmingham

SHIPWRECK DISASTER

It was a disaster, my ship had crashed on a nice but mysterious thingy. Absolutely no one else was on this thingy. Anything at any time could happen good or bad. The best that ever happened to me was that time when I had the ability to catch fish. Now I am never hungry because I caught loads of fish. Enough about food because … my ship's broken, now how am I supposed to escape this island without my ship?

Jake Harris (9)
Woodthorpe Primary School, Birmingham

THE SHIPWRECK THAT CAUSED A LOT OF TROUBLE

I learnt Arabic and how to write in that language. But how was I going to get out of here? No ships were around to see us two (my friend and I). I was starving. There was no food and I hadn't had any for hours. My friend was also starving and very hungry. The only water was the ocean and it was way too salty. We could only drink 3% of it.

Thomas Llewellyn (9)
Woodthorpe Primary School, Birmingham

THE EGYPT DISCOVERY

Carefully, I took a step down the stairs. It felt like I was never going to reach the bottom. There were creaking noises with each step I took. Exhausted and tired, I didn't know if I could make it. As I was going down the stairs I saw a flash of light so I rushed further, almost stumbling. There was a door so I opened it. To my surprise I found myself in a tomb!

Ahmed Chohan (9)
Woodthorpe Primary School, Birmingham

THE HUNT FOR THE DIAMONDS

I was running quickly thinking I'd get caught. I found it – the temple of never return, I ran in realising that there were traps everywhere. Then I became more cautious. Suddenly two Aztec hunters jumped at me so I got my knife and stabbed them both dead.
After a while I found the diamonds, I grabbed them and ran. Suddenly a giant ball came rolling after me. Then I saw the end and jumped out the way.

Ammar Ali (9)
Woodthorpe Primary School, Birmingham

THE ADVENTURE

I stretched my arm as far as it would go. I had been doing it for hours. My legs started to ache so I sat down and munched an apple. I put my sore feet up on a small piece of wood and stopped to breathe in the fresh air. I carried on climbing and grabbing wooden pieces. I wondered if I would ever make it to the top. Finally the canopy surrounded me. I had made it.

Seren Hazel Gallagher (9)
Woodthorpe Primary School, Birmingham

THE BLEEDING FINGER

I walked slowly down the stairs, feeling extremely tired. Soon I reached the bottom where there was a door that I opened. I quickly ran into the huge room and saw tombs of mummies. I decided to open one and remove a bandage to put onto my finger; which stopped it from bleeding immediately. I decided to get out quickly in case one of the mummies woke up. I zoomed up the winding stairs, until I saw daylight from outside.

Isobel MacLennan (9)
Woodthorpe Primary School, Birmingham

UNTITLED

On the tropical island of Hawaii, a surf tournament took place. To his amazement, one surfer did a 360. He didn't know that the pattern on the back of his board was a curse. The longer he spent surfing, the more the magic made the volcano erupt. Petrified, the villagers ran for their lives. Unaware of the spell, the surfer rode the waves. Everyone had to evacuate. The volcano was blasting out red steaming hot lava everywhere.

Keeley Harris (10)
Woodthorpe Primary School, Birmingham

THE ICELAND

I went on a journey to Iceland, I travelled on a furry polar bear. It was very cold and very quickly darkness fell. I made an igloo. The first thing I had was fish for my supper. The catch was delicious. Tired and weary, I slept. The next day I went for a walk. Suddenly the ice cracked. I thought I was going to die. I jumped out of the way and ran back to the igloo.

Megan Crompton (9)
Woodthorpe Primary School, Birmingham

Young Writers Information

We hope you have enjoyed reading this book - and that you will continue to enjoy it in the coming years.

If you like reading and creative writing drop us a line, or give us a call, and we'll send you a free information pack.

Alternatively if you would like to order further copies of this book or any of our other titles, then please give us a call or log onto our website at www.youngwriters.co.uk

Young Writers Information
Remus House
Coltsfoot Drive
Peterborough
PE2 9BF
(01733) 890066